Published in Grenada by Sail Rock Publishing
ISBN 978-976-95346-1-2

Cover Design and Illustrations ©Sandra Preisig

 www.fidelproductions.com

Sustainable Forestry Initiative® (SFI®) Certified Sourcing.
Forest Stewardship Council™ (FSC®) Mix Credit. FSC® C084699

The Flying Falcones

A Novella

by Susan Payetta

for Flossy

Prologue

Lina did something today that she's not accustomed to. She sat with a group of strangers and ate lunch. And dessert! Lina often forgets to eat lunch, and when she does remember to grab a sandwich from the deli, she eats alone at her desk. Now she can't figure out if she was supposed to go back to her room or hang around here in the hospital dining room. This *is* a hospital, isn't it? Why else would that doctor keep popping in to visit? He *said* he was a doctor, although Lina knows he's really a spy. Bond, Doctor Bond. Claimed to be some kinda specialist—with a special interest in gerontology, and he asked her a lot of stupid questions.

"Oh, yeah? Well, I got a special interest in the circus," Lina told him when he insisted on keeping up the ruse, "but that don't make me a clown!"

Lina wanders into the big room at the end of the hall where most of the other patients are either fast asleep or in a coma. She sees one of those "personal care workers" pushing a wheelchair out into the hallway. She looks like a *nurse* to Lina, although definitely not the way nurses used to look since they started wearing pajamas to work. And they all talk to her like she's a retard. Lina catches up with the fake nurse, the one who told her they were going to do something very interesting this afternoon, although Lina can't remember what the hell it was that was supposed to be so interesting. Lina takes a look at the body in the wheelchair and sees the woman she shares a room with. *Never seen her awake yet*, Lina thinks, and asks the "nurse" when the hell they're going to start serving lunch?

"Mrs. Falcone! We just finished lunch! Don't forget about the special movie matinée! We'll start as soon as I take Mildred back to her room!" she hollers.

"I'm not deaf, *nurse!*" Lina yells back. "Might as well take her to the morgue. She already checked out."

"Oh, you're quite a card aren't you, Mrs. Falcone? I'm Sharon. I think you'll like the movie, it's about the circus! Now you wait here and I'll be back in a jiffy!"

The circus? Lina has a special interest in the circus.

The movie is that one where Burt Lancaster and Tony Curtis are both in love with Gina Lollobrigida. *Trapeze*, a three-act. That's where Lina got the idea for her sister Tessa's best costume.

Lina studied the posters at the movie theatre when they all travelled to Palermo for a gig. The film had been running non-stop since its release in 1956. It was the first time Lina had been away from home, and between the train and the ferry, the trip seemed to take forever. Sicily was like a foreign country to them. Lina made some sketches and notes, then stitched Tessa's costume together when they got back to Calabria on the mainland.

Lina and Giuseppe had been going together for a few years before her sister Tessa met Giuseppe's brother Francis. Of course Tessa had seen them perform. *The Flying Falcone Brothers* were the most famous aerialists in Calabria. Actually, they were the only aerialists in Calabria, but they were pretty famous, too. Francis took one look at Tessa and it was love at first sight. At Lina and Giuseppe's wedding, Tessa caught the bouquet. Then Francis got the idea to turn their two-act into a three-act, which was all the rage in Italian circus in those days. At first Giuseppe was against it, but Francis kept after him until Giuseppe agreed to give Tessa a try. She was a natural. It was love at first flight. Then she married Francis and they became *The Flying Falcones*.

Giuseppe and Francis worked Tessa like a dog. She was a fast learner and everybody said she looked just like Gina Lollobrigida, especially after she got a pixie cut. Then she was a dead ringer.

It wasn't supposed to be their final performance. Some bigshot from Montreal was going to be in the audience that night and they wanted to impress him. Their big break, that's what it was supposed to be. But Tessa wasn't back into shape after the twins were born. Their timing was off, the brothers said, although Lina knew it was the extra weight. *Huomo!* What did they think? Tessa could just spit out a couple babies and go right back to work? Giuseppe said it was okay. He had been bulking up while they were off, and if he could catch Franny, he'd have no trouble catching Tessa. She didn't weight 90 lbs. soaking wet and Giuseppe was the best catcher in the business. And better looking than Burt Lancaster, as far as Lina was concerned. "*Piacere, Contessa! It's only one show,*" Francis begged her. Then they'd sign a contract with the man from Montreal and move to Canada.

"Would you pipe down! We're trying to watch the movie here!"

9

Lina is startled. She didn't realise she was talking out loud. "Oh shut up, you old geezer. Don't worry, I'm leaving!" she says.

One of the Sharons says, "You don't have to leave, Mrs. Falcone. Just please be quiet so the others can watch the movie, okay?"

So Lina let out the seams in Tessa's best costume. She even put in a gusset, but it was still too tight. Tessa complained that she could hardly breathe. Lina still has Tessa's costumes tucked away. She gets up to go look at them before she realises she's not in her house, the duplex Giuseppe and Francis built.

"Would you sit down, Falcone! I can't see!"

"I seen it before. Burt Lancaster gets the girl." Lina scowls and shuffles back to her room.

In those days Italian circuses had the worst reputation on the planet. Anyone who could swing it went to Marseille or Paris. But the competition was fierce and they didn't have the money to traipse around Europe looking for work. So that was the plan: start a new life in Canada and get out of that stinking place for good. Their big break, that's what it was supposed to be.

Lina's roommate is asleep, or they haven't been around to collect the body yet. Lina lies down on the other bed and thinks about the circus. When was that? The late sixties, early seventies? It seems so vivid to her now, Lina can practically smell it. Could be the popcorn they're serving with the movie, or more likely it's because her room is so close to the toilets it smells like elephant shit. Those were the days. The four of them were a team. Lina was manager and handled all the business for *The Flying Falcones*, the greatest aerialists in all of Italy! They were young and had their whole lives spread out in front of them. Now they're all dead, except Lina.

Lina doesn't like to reminisce about the days when Giuseppe was working so hard at the family business he never had any time for her. It only makes her miss him, and no amount of wishing will bring him back. It got to the point where Giuseppe wasn't interested in anything outside of work. All those sleepless nights spent "sexually frustrated in a devitalized marriage," according to Dr. Phil. Another fake, that one. Lina was frustrated alright, sitting alone in her sewing room after being rejected in the bedroom. She was in her prime, her body was still firm and her hair was chestnut brown, according to Miss Clairol. Even that old bag wouldn't dispute it's the colour of putty, now.

Giuseppe's sex drive was so low they rarely made love. Lina tried everything she could think of to get Giuseppe more interested in her, which only ended up making her feel less desirable and more miserable when he refused her advances. Her biological clock was ticking like a terrorist's underwear. If it wasn't for that incident with Francis, Lina might have remained barren. A very likely possibility, now that she knows what all those cigarettes were doing to Giuseppe. If they only knew then, what they know now. SMOKING CAUSES IMPOTENCE. It says so, right there on the package. In the end, Lina knew the cigarettes killed Giuseppe. His lungs were shot and he was so short of breath he could barely climb the stairs.

The incident, as Lina prefers to call it, happened long before it got that bad, way back when Franny's perpetual grief was so overwhelming, she couldn't stand it anymore. The entire household was larded with misery. Something needed to be done. Giuseppe refused to talk to Francis about it; the brothers barely spoke to each other outside of work. Except for sausage, of course–always with the sausage! Giuseppe and Francis never talked about anything *emotional*. They blamed each other for what happened to Tessa, and never agreed about whose fault it was.

Francis needed a woman's company. He needed to share his feelings about losing Tessa and Lina had needs, too. It didn't take much to ignite a fire that neither of them could put out. Lina was frantic when she thought she might be pregnant after their tryst in the attic one night while Giuseppe was working late. She made an extra special effort to seduce Giuseppe–quite successfully with the help of... what do they call those thingamajigs again? Never mind, she got the job done just in case she was pregnant and so she wouldn't have to convince her husband that it was an immaculate conception. When John was born exactly nine months later, who would have guessed that he might've been a couple weeks late? At least that's what Lina believes, and who's left to argue about it?

That's really what killed Franny. When Lina got pregnant, Francis was worried to death that Giuseppe would find out about their one-night affair. Nobody knew he had congenital heart disease. When Giuseppe confronted Francis about something or other–something that had nothing to do with it–Francis got so worked up his ticker couldn't take it and wham, bam, thank-you Fran. Franny had left the building.

"Where the hell am I?" Lina shouts at the woman in the other bed. No answer. The hospital, she remembers. But why? Lina's not sick, that's for sure. These drugs are clouding her head and making her forget stuff. And God knows what they're putting in the food, she's not as horny as she used to be. Lina's tired now. When John gets here she'll make him take her home so she can look for Tessa's costumes. There's something important about those costumes. Lina tries to recall what it is, as she drifts off into a drug-induced slumber.

The minute the rush dies down at Falcone Fine Foods, Rosemarie Catanzaro takes a half-empty tray of souvlaki into the walk-in cooler. "Ciao, Cinghiali," she quips as she passes the suspended and inert bodies of two wild boars. She begins to refill her tray and hears grunting. Rosemarie's eyes grow wide as she backs away from the carcasses. *Maybe those pigs aren't dead yet?* She glances up and sees Randy the butcher thrusting his hips... *it can't be!* Rosemarie has heard about some farm boys with uncontrollable urges around livestock, but to actually witness *bestiality?* She lets out a little squeal and retreats from the cooler in shock.

In spite of the low temperature, her face burns with embarrassment. Rosemarie is caught between the walk-in cooler and the customer service area, stranded in the meat cutting room, when a woman she's never seen before barges through the double doors to confront her. Rosemarie wonders if she's a customer. She's not wearing a uniform and has a crazed, angry look on her face. The stranger is armed with a large *soppressata* and prepares to launch it at Rosemarie's head.

Instinctively, Rosemarie hoists the pan of souvlaki to parry the thrust of the giant salami. A shower of bite-size pieces of marinated meat rain down, causing Rosemarie's assailant to slip on the oily floor. Like the memory of a happier day for the two witnesses hanging on the nearby meat hooks, she wallows in the marinade while Rosemarie escapes.

Randy chases Rosemarie. He begs her to slow down while he smooths out his curly red hair and fumbles to retie his apron. Rosemarie pushes through the double doors of the meat cutting room into another throng of hungry customers who are crammed in front of the meat display cases, shouting for service. Randy hurries through the cooler door and slides to a stop when he sees his wife on the floor. Lightly seasoned with olive oil, garlic, salt, pepper and just enough acidic lemon juice to blind her, she doesn't see him. Randy steps gingerly over his wife's body and skates through the double doors behind Rosemarie, reciting his standard incantation, "I can help who's next. I don't know who's next?"

Tiffany takes her time to tidy up a bit. She tucks long strands of blonde hair back into her hairnet and replaces her *Falcone* cap. Tiffany steps out from behind the wild boars hanging in the cooler, selects a case of pickerel fillets–the lightest box she could have chosen–and rejoins the mayhem.

Randy smirks as Tiffany glides past him with a glisten in her eye and that unmistakable just-been-fucked look on her face. "I thought I smelled fish," Randy says.

Transfixed by the shocking discovery of her co-workers caught *in flagrante delicto*, Rosemarie stands alongside Randy assessing the situation until a customer breaches her trance.

"Can I get some service? Hey, bella! Who do you gotta know around this joint to get some service?"

"Sure. I mean yes, sir. What can I get for you today?" Rosemarie stutters while she watches Randy saunter off.

"Gimme a couple Dog Lake Specials and do you have any of that good Italian sausage? The dry-cured *Toscano*?"

"I'm afraid the *cinghiale* isn't ready yet." Rosemarie selects two large steaks, throws them onto the scale and punches in the code for sirloin–*18*? Rosemarie just started working at Falcone last week and she hasn't memorized the product codes yet. She tears off a large piece of butcher wrap and asks, "Would you like these marinated?"

"What are you, new here?"

"As a matter of fact I am," *and I haven't cracked the Falcone Code yet*, she wants to add, but doesn't.

"Ask the butcher," the customer snaps. "He knows the deal."

"He's a bit busy."

"Better be makin' the *cinghiale*," the smartass says.

"It has to do with sausage, that's for sure. Hang on. I'll get him for you."

Rosemarie peers through the windows in the double doors to the meat cutting room which is sandwiched between the customer service area and the walk-in cooler. The crazed woman has vanished and so has Randy. Rosemarie proceeds with caution through the slippery mess and out a side door to the receiving area. She spots them out on the loading dock. Judging by the way the woman is sobbing and whacking at Randy, Rosemarie figures that she must be his wife. Rosemarie quietly returns to the front of the house.

"Sorry, he must have stepped out," Rosemarie tells the

customer. "But I can call John for you. I think he's downstairs in his office."

"Just put some steak spice on 'em and vacuum pack 'em. I'm in a hurry. And for chrissake, tell Johnny to teach you how to do your job so I don't have to, will ya? They should be at least two inches thick. Old Man Falcone would be spinning in his grave if he saw these scrawny little things."

***

"How was work?" Rosemarie's mother asks with as much interest as she can feign. Through the phone line, Rosemarie can tell that her mother is multitasking. She hears water running and pictures an ice-cream scoop being rinsed.

"Exhausting. I can't believe I'm starting over at my age. It's very demanding physically, and the goddamn *Falcone Code* is harder to crack than the da Vinci code." Rosemarie would like to speak with the person who wrote the product code for the scales. She was told to have it memorized within two weeks and she's having a difficult time. Besides that, Rosemarie discovered that if she puts the same sausage on a different scale, it uses a different code number. Whoever wrote that cursed code has a sick sense of humour.

"Don't swear, *Rosamarina*. Your father, God rest his soul, never liked it, and neither do I."

"Sorry, Ma. Anyhow, at least I don't have to go to the gym anymore. Even if I had the energy for it, I can't afford it. And I'm getting a good workout, especially on the closing-shift. Jesus... *sorry*, we have to take the whole place apart, wrap all the meat and put it away in the cooler, then clean everything from top to bottom. I'm thirty-three years old and working with a bunch of teenagers who *have* a life. They want to get out of there as soon as they can, so they go full tilt."

"Well, you can't blame them," her mother says through a mouthful of something crunchy. Most likely an ice cream cone, possibly *cantucci*, or maybe *biscotti*. Definitely something sweet. Her mother has a passion for sugar and often skips dinner to get to the "main event."

"I know, but just because I don't have a life, doesn't mean I have a clean enough conscience to do a lousy job. I take food-safety very seriously, you know."

"Of course you do, but they're just kids. They don't know any better."

"You got that right, Ma. I had to show one of those kids how to sweep the floor!"

Mervin had been flicking crap all over the cabinet Rosemarie had just wiped down. He was shocked when Rosemarie grabbed the broom from him and unearthed a few stray sausages and bits and pieces of wrappings from under the counter.

"He thanked me for the demonstration and claimed he didn't think the broom would reach under the counter!"

"See. He's trying."

Great, now she's sticking up for that lunatic.

"When I asked Mervin why he had a pair of gloves hanging out of his back pocket instead of on his hands, he told me he likes to keep them handy. He said he didn't need them because his hands were really clean since he washed them about a million times."

"We always wear gloves when we make sandwiches for funerals at the church," Rosemarie's mother states.

"Yeah? Well, that's great. You wouldn't want to kill somebody at a funeral."

In Rosemarie's opinion, gloves provide a false sense of cleanliness. She thinks it would be better if the public knew how easy it is for food service workers to forget they're wearing gloves while serving food. Their hands feel perfectly clean inside a glove that's been places they'd never stick a bare hand. Rosemarie caught herself using her gloved-hand to pick up something that fell on the floor earlier today. As she tossed the food into the garbage can, she remembered to toss the glove, too. Had she not been wearing gloves, she would have instinctively known to wash her hands immediately. Good thing John Falcone doesn't mind if she uses a hundred gloves per day.

"I'm sorry you had a bad day, *ragazza*. I had a good day. I won eighty-three dollars, and your sister lost at least that much, so there you go."

"How much did you spend before you scored?" It's not that Rosemarie cares how her mother spends her money; she wants her to understand that she never really *wins* at the casino. Her sister Roseanna, can afford that kind of "entertainment" with Eddy sending cheques home from Alberta every two weeks. She's fixed for life. Eddy makes a fortune working as a high-rigger and Roseanna has never had to work a day in her life, motherhood notwithstanding. Four in a row, and to hear her tell it, she's only had sex four times.

"Not much, not today. Today was a good day."

"Well, that makes one of us. I gotta go, Ma. I'm tired. I'll call you again soon."

"Okay, I'll see you Sunday. Why don't you bring that Brian along. We haven't seen him in ages."

That Brian. "Brian and I aren't seeing each other right now. We're taking a break." That's the way *he* put it. Rosemarie is not so sure they should have stayed together as long as they did.

"Oh. I see." Her mother never liked Brian and Brian wasn't too fond of Rosemarie's family either. He never wanted to go to her mom's house for Sunday dinner. *Too ethnic,* he said.

"Well, don't work too hard. And don't take it all on your shoulders. You're only one person. And it won't be forever, *chica,* you'll see. A pretty girl like you, you'll get your life back."

"Thanks, Ma. Love you."

"*Buona notte*, Rosamarina."

Rosemarie's life, as she knows it, is over. She certainly hopes she doesn't have to use her good looks to get her life back. Rosemarie is confident that her skills and experience should be enough to open whatever doors need opening, even though she may have to do a bit of barging now that most of those doors have been locked from the inside.

Rosemarie knows that beauty can be a curse. While she attended Lakehead University, she deliberately dressed in clothes that didn't flatter her petite figure or draw attention to her pretty face. She wanted to project a completely different image than the one she had grown up with. She was as sick of being called "the pretty one," as her sister was of being called "the athletic one." Neither of them was ever called "the smart one," something that bugged both of them. So when Rosemarie started university, she wore baggy overalls and rubber boots, pulled her dirty-blonde hair back into a ragged ponytail—anything she could do to keep the boys at bay and keep her focussed on her studies. She wanted to be taken seriously.

As Rosemarie matured and established a name for herself in the business world she was finally able to dress the part of a successful career woman. She affected a very feminine look to counter her hard-core attitude toward business. Rosemarie took great care with her wardrobe. She paid extra attention to details like accessories, and footwear in particular. She wore her hair in a bob, cut every six weeks by Mr. Maurice. To his dismay, Rosemarie kept her natural honey colour without the aid of dye and only allowed him to add a bit of shine using a product so expensive it came in a tiny glass bottle that dispensed one precious drop at a time. Rarely was Rosemarie seen with her hair pulled back or pinned up, unless she was at the gym. She wouldn't be caught at a dog fight without make-up. Those days are done.

Rosemarie's car insurance is due at the end of the month—which doesn't matter because her car will be repossessed when she can't make the payments—and she has no idea how the hell she's going to pay the rent. The only asset Rosemarie owns is a collection of ridiculously expensive shoes, which probably won't fit her swollen crippled feet ever again. Rosemarie has got to get some new runners, but her credit card's maxed and her debit card's useless, so she'll have to make do until payday. Her Reeboks were fine for the gym, but eight or nine hours in those meat-slippers and her toes are throbbing.

There's no way Rosemarie is going to ask Brian to lend her

some cash. Even if she did ask, he'd probably refuse. Brian is always giving Rosemarie the gears about her spending. As an investment adviser, Brian makes loads of the stuff and his expense account covers all the things that Rosemarie has to fork out real money for. Things like dining out and putting gas in the car. Quite nervy of Brian, considering it was always him going on about how Rosemarie needs to project the right image. And of course that image included all those things that Brian was so impressed with: the designer shoes and bags, the fancy car, he even convinced her to join the most expensive health club instead of working out at the Canada Games Complex where she used to go before they met. Come to think of it, the only money Brian ever spent on her came right off his expense account.

She wasn't his girlfriend, she was an asset.

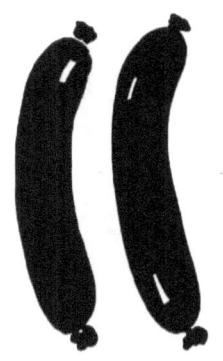

Rosemarie smells marijuana. She punches the clock and washes her hands in preparation for another day that promises to be as gruelling as the last. Rosemarie checks out her co-workers, but nobody else seems to notice the skunky scent that permeates the atmosphere. Perhaps some sniffers aren't as sensitive as Rosemarie's. Or could it be that Rosemarie's colleagues don't know what pot smells like? That's a real possibility; they're all fairly buttoned-down.

Gord sashays past Rosemarie, leaving another waft of weed in his wake. He's singing and looks far too happy for a guy who's here to pick up the orders for delivery. *So, Gord's a stoner?* A middle-aged straight guy who sings show tunes for chrissake, Rosemarie should have known. And that song he's belting out now, "*... When something's done wrong, what can I say, someone could send me home today. I'm making minimum wage!*"

When Rosemarie asks Gord what he's singing, he looks at her as if she just arrived from outer space. "BusBoys," Gord says and proceeds to give Rosemarie the extended version of the all black rock 'n roll band's CV and discography. "It was a minor hit back in the early 80's. Topped the charts in the Twin Cities, though," Gord claims. "Ground breaking stuff. Bunch of brothers singing butt bumpin' rock 'n roll." *Well, give me a toke of whatever he's smoking and let's get lost in the 80's!*

"Morning, Rose. Are you serving?" John asks.

"Not at the moment, boss, I just came in. You want me to do something?" This is Rosemarie's second week on the job and she's having a hard time getting used to thinking of her former schoolmate as her boss. She's known John since they were kids.

"Yeah, hon. Can you give Gord a hand with the order for the Scand? He's gotta get it there by ten."

Yahoo! "Sure, no problem," Rosemarie says, hoping she'll get to tag along on the delivery to the Scandinavian Home Café.

"All this ground beef has to be wrapped in two pound packs." John drops a huge bin on the counter behind Rosemarie. He grabs a handful of medium-ground and forms a softball-size meatball. "Just make a bunch of balls like this, then wrap them and put them into that box. It's marked. We need another 27."

So, no delivery. Just more meat. And calling her *hon.* Rosemarie didn't think anybody got away with that sort of language anymore, but it's like they're stuck in a time-warp around here.

Rosemarie wraps the ground beef as fast as she can. She constantly has to check the weight on the scale because she can't tell how much two pounds feels like. She has organized a parade of giant meatballs marching alarmingly close to the deli end of the twenty-foot meat counter. That's a no-no. Fresh meat cannot come into contact with cold cuts. Rosemarie loses track of the count again. She is recounting the packages when Carol slips past her to wash her hands.

Carol has worked for the Falcone family since they opened in the 70's. She has a slight, wiry build. She's wound so tight she could snap in half in a good breeze. Though Carol is not officially part of management, she designated herself as Rosemarie's supervisor after John introduced them. Rosemarie suspects that Carol enjoys having someone new to boss around. Sometimes, Rosemarie gets the feeling Carol is trying to belittle her and wonders if Carol knows about Rosemarie's recent fall from grace at the school board.

"Always serve customers while you're putting up orders," Carol instructs.

Rosemarie glances up and sees a customer that she hadn't noticed until now. *Where did Carol go?* "Hi. What can I get for you today?" Rosemarie asks.

The customer tells Rosemarie he's not sure what he wants yet. He is still deciding when John comes flying out of nowhere.

"Hey, buddy, how ya doin'? Need some help?" John turns to Rosemarie and says, "Always greet the customer, Rose."

"No, I'm good," the customer tells John.

When the customer finally decides he wants two hundred grams of mortadella sliced, Rosemarie says, "I'll just wash my hands and be right with you."

"Good girl. How's that order coming? Gord's gotta go. You know what? I'll finish it up," John says, all in one breath.

Micromanagement, that's John Falcone. It's a wonder he gets anything done. The next customer is already bending his ear about a fishing trip to Lac des Mille Lac when Gord comes back looking for the Scand's order. He's still singing, *"... I said that I work for minimum wage!"* and Rosemarie thinks he looks pretty happy for a guy earning $10.25 per hour. *How can he afford the stuff?*

"How's the fishing up there?" John asks the customer while he watches Gord whisk away the box of meat.

"Oh, it don't matter. All that meat and a boatload of booze, who cares if they're biting? Mostly we just catch and release. It's more about being out in the bush with your buddies, eh?"

"I hear ya, buddy. How do these steaks look?"

"Beauty. Thanks, Johnny, you're the best. Whadaya got planned yourself this weekend?"

"Pretty much here," John says without any sign of disappointment.

"Yeah? Well, somebody's gotta work. See you when hunting season opens."

Rosemarie slices the mortadella very carefully, trying to get it as thin as she can. She turns the thickness dial down another notch and now she's only getting half slices.

John watches her. "Hey, Rosie, you have to try to keep the slices whole without shaving them. Let me show you." Rosemarie steps aside while John adjust the thickness ever so slightly. "You have to catch the slices before they fall, then flip them onto the paper. Lay them out like this in one layer, put paper between every layer."

"Okay, John. Thanks." Rosemarie tries to copy John's technique. It looks a mess. When Rosemarie puts the heap on the scale John is right beside her again.

"Sorry, buddy," John says to the customer. He lifts an entire layer off the top and says, "We're a bit over, but you know what? I'll give you a better deal." John punches in the code for San Danielle (*2, Rosemarie notes. Lean is 3, 4 is hot*). He prints the label, drops the *free* layer of cold cuts back on the heap, folds it over neatly and slips it into a sandwich bag, sticking the label across the end to seal it. One smooth move. "Sorry for the wait," John says and hands the guy the best deal he's probably ever had.

"Thanks for your patience," Rosemarie says, "I just started working here and I'm still in training."

"Good job, Rosie," John says. "You'll get the hang of it. I can tell you're a quick learner."

It's August and it's hot. The humidity is so high, condensation fills the evaporator pan that threatens to overflow and drip onto the deli products. And it's only quarter after ten. It's going to be one of those crazy summer days. Nobody wants to stay indoors and cook when it's this hot. A barbecue-rush can last late into the evening because the store doesn't close until nine-thirty during the summer. Rosemarie is supposed to get off at six, which is fortunate because she doesn't think she could take another closing-shift tonight. Last night Rosemarie didn't get home until a few minutes before midnight and was so keyed up she didn't get to sleep until after three. She feels like she just left this place.

"Rose, can you wash the lettuce, then rinse the spinner? It goes by the vacuum packer when you're done. I'm going out for a quick smoke," Carol says, before she disappears again. *No wonder she's so wrinkled*, Rosemarie thinks.

If it weren't for the wrinkles Rosemarie might like to take up smoking herself. The smokers always seem to get more breaks.

Rosemarie came in at two o'clock the day before and she didn't get her first break until after six. It was so busy Rosemarie had no time to clean anything until they locked the doors at nine-thirty. She never got a chance to take her second break.

Rosemarie has washed a mountain of lettuce and filled the food pans for sandwiches when Carol comes back.

"Fill the counter between customers," Carol says. "We need fryers. They're in the cooler by the olives. Use six-pound bags."

The walk-in cooler is a cornucopia of meat. Rosemarie has yet to work out how it's organized so she feels useless and confused. She tries to figure out where the chickens are but can't even find any olives. Finally the low temperature forces her into action. She locates the olives and looks behind them. Pork chops. Eventually, Rosemarie finds stacks of boxes labelled with every cut of chicken except the one she needs. No whole chickens, no broilers, no fryers. She's about to give up when Randy enters the cooler. Rosemarie is relieved to see that he left the door ajar.

"Whatcha lookin' for, darlin'?"

"Whole chickens. Carol says they're by the olives."

"She don't know squat," Randy says. He points to the bottom shelf behind the stack of boxes Rosemarie just rifled through. "Don't think she's been in here in over a decade."

Rosemarie struggles to extricate the chickens from their hiding place without toppling the adjacent and unstable stack of chicken parts.

"Need a hand with that, darlin'?"

"No thanks, I think I can manage, Randy,"

"Well, look at the gunners on you!" Randy grabs a handful of ground pork from the meat grinder that lives in the cooler and leaves without hearing Rosemarie say, "I'd appreciate it if you stopped calling me *darlin'*."

Juggling six chickens by the legs, three in each hand, Rosemarie works out her own system for memorizing the codes. *Chicken 101; whole fryers. 102; breasts—two breasts per chicken? That'll work. 103; legs—three-legged chicken race? 104; wings—every chicken has four wings if you count the flat and the drummie! 105; boneless breasts...* she's stuck.

Rosemarie bags the whole chickens and stretches to place them into the display case. She looks through the glass front and sees the first bun-wielding customer of the day approach the counter. Customers can choose their own bun from the bins up front and bring it to the deli to have a sandwich custom-made.

"Can I get a sandwich?" a young woman with flaming auburn hair asks.

"Sure, I'll just wash my hands," Rosemarie says like it's her hobby. "Would you like mustard, mayo, lettuce, tomato?"

"Everything but mayo. I'll have sun-dried tomato-basil turkey breast with creamy havarti."

Figures. Both of those products are very difficult to slice; the cheese is soft, which puts resistance on the blade, and the turkey is slippery and oddly shaped so it doesn't sit firmly under the pusher block. Rosemarie was alarmed when she saw one of her co-workers use her fingers instead of the pusher block to steady the turkey one day. When Rosemarie mentioned the inherent risk of the product slipping, the silly woman claimed she had a good two inches between her and the blade, and looked at Rosemarie like she was Elmer the

Safety Elephant. Rosemarie couldn't watch, afraid she'd jinx her.

Rosemarie is not willing to risk her fingertips for some skinny chick's sandwich, so she clandestinely cranks the carriage width up a couple of notches and quickly cuts a few thick slices.

"Can you slice that a little thinner, *puhlease?*" the customer-who-thinks-she's-eating-diet-food asks.

"No problem," Rosemarie replies stone-faced. A lie, if ever she told one. She finishes making the sandwich, wraps it and tosses it onto the scale. Regardless of what goes in, sandwiches are all priced by the weight using code 96, tax exempt if they're under four dollars. This one is a bargain at only $3.15.

No one in their right mind would shop at Falcone if they were really on a diet. There's nothing remotely healthy here, Rosemarie thinks, *except maybe the sun-dried tomato-basil turkey breast.* Rosemarie doesn't even know what it tastes like, she hates it so much already. *And there's probably about a million calories in that stupid cheese!* Before she started working at Falcone, Rosemarie never knew so many people ate havarti, outside of Denmark that is, but it's their top-selling cheese, at least in sandwiches. *Probably because nobody wants to slice it themselves at home.*

Another item that flies off the shelf is Falcone's Italian sausage. Mild, medium or hot, Falcone sells sausage like nobody's business. It's their specialty and they've been making it exactly the same way for generations. Two, for sure.

John's Uncle Francis started the business with John's mom and dad when they emigrated from the old country. The three F's intermingled on the company logo originally represented Francis, Giuseppe and Lina. John's mom, Lina was an equal partner from the beginning and still owns one-third. When John's dad, Giuseppe died, John inherited his share. When Francis died, his twin boys inherited his share. As is customary with twins in too many ways, Frankie and Nick split Francis' share equally. The same way they shared birthdays, confirmations and graduations; every milestone and achievement had to be celebrated collectively. After Giuseppe died, John took over management. Lina still does the bookkeeping. Although John's cousins both work in the store, only Nick plays a small managerial role as supervisor of the evening shift. Frankie's commitment and loyalty to the family business is steadfast, though he prefers to avoid responsibility for any decision making.

Rosemarie remembers coming here with her dad on Saturday afternoons when she was a kid. A little bell tinkled as they stepped into the tiny store in the front of the old Falcone family home on Connie Street. The sawdust covered wood floor creaked as they made their way through the maze of fascinating foreign objects hung from the ceiling. That was back when they got away without refrigerating dry-cured salami. The smell remains vivid in Rosemarie's memory. A blend of dirty socks and rotten tomatoes, accented with a top note of cigarette smoke. The old man's squint-eyed countenance, a result of the rollie that dangled in perpetuity from his lip while he worked, is a creepy reminder of the days when smoke billowed from every business in town. The intrepid customer who might have thought to complain, would have been "asked" to take their business elsewhere. A transistor radio tuned to CBC, broadcast "Saturday Afternoon at the Opera" live from the Met, and competed for airtime with the customers speaking rapid Italian.

Things have changed. Falcone Fine Foods neither sounds nor

smells like it used to. Everyone speaks English now and classic rock is piped in through a quadraphonic sound system. The health inspector has put an end to meat and cheese products hung from the ceiling, their scents hermetically sealed in plastic and safe from airborne bacteria. And nobody smokes indoors anywhere anymore. But it's still a store of a different colour. No other place compares. And that's the secret to Falcone's success.

John has modernized and expanded the store, adding a self-serve olive bar and all sorts of gourmet food products that bring in the yuppies and people with lots of money to spend on treats. The real Italians don't shop here, not like they used to. When they do come to shop, they buy the Italian specialty products that are vacuum-packed and displayed in self-serve coolers that line the walls all the way from the meat department at the back, to the bakery display at the front of the store. Customers can bag their own bread and buns from open bins, replenished several times a day by the bakeries' own delivery trucks. The southern Italians tend to choose Roma Bakery products, while northern Italians usually opt for Nucci's. Whether their ancestors hail from the slopes of the Dolomites or the toe of the boot, all the Italian customers by-pass Falcone's produce section, which is more of a convenience than anything else for those who don't want to venture out to the big supermarkets where they could find a better selection at a fraction of the price. No self-respecting *paesano* would pay that kind of money for a tomato!

Besides the standard Italian cheeses, Falcone stock a vast selection of gourmet cheese from around the world: everything from Stinking Bishop to halvah, all ignored by the folks who come for asiago, Parmigiano-Reggiano, Romano ... the usual suspects. Then there's the cacciatore, casalinga, pancetta and other pre-packaged dry-cured meats for customers to take home without having to line up in front of the deli. *Italianos* rarely bother with anything that isn't self-serve, except for the precious Prosciutto di Parma and mortadella, of course. Oh, they buy their sausage here when they run out of their own homemade links, or when there's *cinghiali* to be had, and then they complain, "It's not like it used to be when Old Man Falcone was making the sausage!" It is in fact exactly the same. John couldn't change it if he tried. To do so would cause a bloody revolution.

When Italian customers do come to shop, and the line-up snakes through the front door, around the perimeter and back to the cash registers at the front, they by-pass it and elbow their way through to the far end of the deli like they have special privileges just because they're Italian. One woman jumped the queue and tried to get Mervin's attention one day. Mervin may not be the sharpest knife in the block but he told the woman she'd have to get in line. She pretended she didn't understand Mervin and tried again. "I justa wanna some *Prosciuto cotto*, slice-a thin, thin," she cried.

"I'm sorry, Miss, but all these people were here before you," Mervin replied. Smooth, that. Mervin calls all women *Miss* regardless of their sometimes advanced age. As a result, all women love Mervin. Well, most of them do. Not that one.

Italianos come out in droves in the summer when they order cases of Roma tomatoes to make *gravy,* and huge boxes of peppers to roast, and grapes to press in the autumn. And God forbid there isn't enough to go around, that's when Falcone Fine Foods looks like it did in the old days. They fight. Escorted by their embarrassed adult children, old women dressed in black argue over a case of vegetables as if the family reputation is at stake. Parking is a nightmare. Old men wearing fedoras back up their ancient half-ton trucks to the loading dock. They block traffic and refuse to move until they get their precious tomatoes, peppers, grapes... whatever. *Look who's a racist now*, Rosemarie thinks, *and these are my own people!*

Just a couple of months ago Rosemarie was fighting racism. She had a great job, a *career*, as Assistant Director of Human Resources with the board of education, with a future so bright she could see her reflection in her boss's shiny pate. She had a sports car that turned mens' heads and a collection of killer heels that had the same effect on women. And a boyfriend. He dumped Rosemarie when he figured she might become a liability.

Because *technically* she quit her job, Rosemarie has to wait for the government to decide whether or not she qualifies for unemployment insurance benefits. Ironically, they don't call it UI anymore, it's *Employment Insurance* now. As if she'd need it if she was *employed*. With no income, no nest egg and a stack of bills due before the "penalty period" ends (not to mention the fact that she's obliged to be "actively seeking work" if she has any chance of collecting EI), Rosemarie was checking the job postings at Service Canada when she ran into her old schoolmate, John Falcone. He was there looking to hire some students to work in the store for the summer and asked Rosemarie what sort of work she was looking for. Rosemarie accidentally said "anything" and now here she is, working at Falcone, waiting for pogey. And all because of a kid's stupid haircut.

It made *The National*, that haircut. "Thunder Bay mom wants answers after teacher's aide chops off son's hair." The kid's mother tried to press charges but the Crown attorney said there were no grounds for criminal charges. Rosemarie suspects it's because the boy is aboriginal. In Rosemarie's opinion, the Crown knew there would be no public support, and even less chance of a conviction.

Rosemarie ignored the school board's wishes, disobeyed a direct order from her boss and suspended the teacher's assistant. Rosemarie wanted to fire the woman because she showed poor judgement. Worse than that, she showed no remorse. In Rosemarie's experience, if the educator couldn't understand what she had done wrong, especially after all the attention the incident garnered, it was inevitable that she would use poor judgement again in the future. But the board had no intention of taking on the union.

Rosemarie argued her point until the board asked for her resignation. She gave it to them along with a speech that will keep her out of every HR department from here to Sault Ste. Marie. She might as well have burned the Mackinaw bridge. The board members are a tight-knit group of the most connected people in town, and Rosemarie accused them of racism. Welcome to the Lakehead, where attitudes haven't changed much since the days of residential schools, and they still believe it was okay to chop the braids off the Indian kids. With a colonial attitude like that, how can they understand what's so manifestly wrong with this incident?

Rosemarie is famished. She looks around for Carol to see if she can take her break and asks if anyone has seen her. No one seems to know where Carol is, so Rosemarie makes herself a sandwich and wanders out toward the loading dock to see if Carol is out having a cigarette. Rosemarie meets John coming upstairs.

"What's up, Rosie?"

"I'm thinking of taking up smoking," she says, deadpan.

"Oh, don't do that," John says with what appears to be genuine concern.

"Have you seen Carol around?"

"Try the office. I think she's doing the orders for tomorrow."

"Thanks. I'm going to take my break now, John."

Rosemarie finds Carol in the staff lunchroom writing up the orders for the next day and calling the bakeries to order buns.

"Hi, Carol."

"You haven't had your break yet?" Carol asks with mild alarm. "What time did you come in?"

"Nine. It's been so busy I haven't had a chance, but I'm starving."

"You have to take your break when you can get it," Carol says as if Rosemarie hadn't worked that out yet. "We usually go in order, first in goes first, and that. Sorry, I kind of forgot about you. Where's Tracey? Didn't she show up yet?"

"No. Didn't you hear? She was slicing sun-dried tomato-basil turkey breast and nearly took her finger off yesterday."

"That twit. I told her to be more careful about a million times. I don't know what goes on in her head."

"Apparently she wasn't using the pusher block."

"Oh, no wonder," Carol says. "That pusher block is so heavy it mashes up the product. You can't slice Prosciuto without mangling it."

"Yeah, we really do need a new slicer." Rosemarie wonders why John wouldn't replace it. He must know that it's better to invest in proper equipment than to risk his employees' safety, not to mention a Workers' Comp claim and the trouble the Health and Safety Inspector can cause if he notices. They can shut a place down for less than that. "Maybe we should tell John, I mean there's a chance he doesn't know how bad it is, right?"

"Of course he knows! He uses the friggin' thing, too!" Carol shouts. "Anyhow, if there's enough money for new equipment, there's enough to pay us all better. Which one would you pick?"

"You're right. What was I thinking?" Rosemarie snarls, tucking into her *soppressata* and gruyere *panino*, thankful she didn't have to pay for the most expensive choice she could have made. Minimum wage and all the salami she can eat.

"Good morning, Rose," Frankie says cheerfully. Or is it Nick? John's twin cousins don't normally work the same shifts as each other so Rosemarie can't tell them apart yet.

"Morning," Rosemarie says without specifying.

"Did you hear about Randy and Gale?"

"What about them?" Rosemarie just saw Randy downstairs in John's office. Randy's wife, Gale, pulled out of the parking lot when Rosemarie came in a few minutes ago, so she assumes Gale dropped Randy off at work.

"Gale caught Randy fooling around. Again. She marched in here with the *evidence*, going on about tone, texture and length... all the things only a professional would know."

Definitely Frankie. According to Nick, Frankie wants nothing to do with managing the family business, he wants to be a hair stylist. Nick told Rosemarie all about it the first time she worked the closing-shift with him. Apparently neither of them are here by choice. Nick says John doesn't have the money to buy them out, so the three of them are stuck here together.

"I saw Randy's wife leave when I came in. She didn't look too happy," Rosemarie says.

"No? Well Randy won't be either. John's going to fire him," Frankie says with what sounds like glee.

"Why? What's up?" Rosemarie's still not sure who knows what.

"For fooling around with that little hottie, Tiffany! He's going to fire her, too. Company policy: no playing hide-the-sausage on Falcone time."

So it's out.

"The really fun part is that Gale thinks it's *you*," Frankie explains. "She was waiting for you to come in, but I took one look at her *evidence* and said, 'Sister, I got two words for you: p*eroxide*.'"

"That's one word, Frankie."

"Yeah, right. So I told her you don't dye your hair. God knows I would love to put some highlights in it for you, doll face. Any time, just say the word. Anyhow, I told her it had to be Tiffany's. *As if* that's her natural colour! Gale's a stylist, you know. What they're teaching on the east coast these days I can't imagine. Maybe Gale missed that day. Or it might have something to do with all that screech she drinks."

"So, you stuck up for me? Thanks, Frankie."

"Yeah, sure. No problem. So Gale blew outta here and let's hope we've seen the back of her. With any luck she's halfway to Halifax by now." Frankie rests his case.

John suddenly appears and they both make themselves look busy.

"Hey, Frankie, can you get a hold of Timo for me? Tell him I need to talk to him. I'll be back in an hour. Morning, Rose. Tiffany won't be in today. Can you get started on sandwich prep? Thanks, hon." Exit John.

Frankie flashes a look at his confidante that says, *I told you so.* He scurries off to call Timo.

Everybody loves Timo. He was John's right hand man till he decided he'd spent too much time in the cooler and not enough time in the bush. Timo doesn't really need to work anymore because he owns half a dozen houses and some apartments, all rented out and bringing in big bucks, according to Frankie. So when Randy came along looking for a job, Timo quit and moved out to the country where sauna, hunting, fishing, drinking, and all other manly pursuits take place. Timo, with the monster truck and camouflage polar fleece. Timo, Finnish-Canadian semi-retired butcher-cum-landlord. Timo, Thunder Bay's most eligible bachelor.

"Yay! Timo's coming back!" Frankie shouts as he puts down the phone. He pumps his fist like he just won the lottery.

Carol walks in. She looks dumbfounded. "Timo's coming back?"

"Apparently, he's going to cover for Randy," Rosemarie tells Carol.

"I hear Tiffany is finished, too. Good riddance. More work is what we're left with. It's quarter to ten and the prep hasn't even been started yet–"

"I finished the lettuce and tomatoes. Do you need me to do something else?" Rosemarie asks.

"I gotta get started on these orders for meat and cheese trays," Carol says, "so you better clean the slicer."

Again. It seems like Rosemarie just finished putting that thing back together and now she has to take it all apart again and fish out those pesky little tomato seeds that get caught under the blade guard. "Okay, Carol. Anything else?" Rosemarie asks with a little less enthusiasm.

"When you're done we need to get the chickens in the oven. Grab ten fryers out of the cooler and season them. Frankie will show you how. Two and a quarter hours at 350," Carol instructs. "Fahrenheit," she adds. She picks up the order book and shows Rosemarie her back.

Who's we?

After the slicer is clean and the sandwich trays are filled, Frankie helps Rosemarie with the chickens. He forces her to use way more seasoning than she thinks necessary. The seasoning is nothing but paprika-coloured salt. Frankie shakes it on so liberally, the raw chickens look sunburnt.

John returns. "Did you get a hold of Timo, Frankie?"

"Yeah. He said he'll be in just as soon as he finds the keys to his truck. He sounds a bit hungover."

"Good," John says.

"Good," he's coming in? or *"good," he's hungover?* Rosemarie wonders.

"I called Tracey. She's our cheese girl, but she can't come in before noon. Frankie show you how to do the chickens, Rose?" John asks.

Cheese Girl? Next thing he'll tell me they've got a Wiener Boy! "Yes, I think I've got it: *thoroughly* seasoned, two per rack, two and a quarter hours at 350. It sure seems like too much salt," Rosemarie says, although Frankie insists that it "cooks off" in the oven.

"Don't worry," John says. "It cooks off in the oven."

Sheesh. The fat might, but Rosemarie knows the salt is headed straight for the arteries. *What's up with these guys?*

"When the birds are done put them into the special barbecue bags. You'll find some by the wrapping machine in the back. And don't forget to label them, then put them in the bottom holding oven," John explains. "You know the code, Rose?"

"101?"

"Nooo," John says, "101's for whole chickens."

Silly me, what was I thinking?

"Frankie! What's the code for barbequed chickens?" John hollers.

"98!"

"Don't worry, Rose. You'll get it," says John, the only one besides her who *doesn't* know the codes. "Frankie, can you call Nick and see if he can come in a little early? We need to have a meeting tonight."

"Sure, John. Me too, or just Nick?"

"You too, Frankie. Big pow wow. The whole board of directors."

The lunch rush was particularly punishing and it's finally time for Rosemarie's break. She glances at the clock and remembers, two and a quarter hours at 350. *Shit!* She runs to the oven and hits the button that she thinks will stop the rotisserie. Whoever designed this oven decorated with little symbols of hands and clocks, must have been a whiz kid in kindergarten. There's some other hieroglyphic markings Rosemarie is uncertain of, but she decides it's better to ignore them than to admit she can't work it out. Square peg, round hole. Rosemarie opens the oven and peers in, fully expecting to find the shrivelled remains of bird-like creatures. But *goddamn it*, if they don't look delicious! All that salt has kept them plump and juicy.

Rosemarie looks for the special heat-proof bags and can't find them among a myriad of packaging. She searches through bags of every shape and size, and finds all the various types of bags except the ones she needs. As Rosemarie straightens her spine, groaning and muttering to herself, she sees Timo, larger than life, watching her.

"Whatcha lookin' for?" Timo asks.

"Barbecue chicken bags. Hi, Timo. Remember me?"

"Under the garbage bags. Yeah, high school. Whatcha doin' here?"

"Looking for bags," Rosemarie says.

"No, I mean whatcha doin' *here*?" Timo clarifies.

"Down and out," she says, without further explanation.

Rosemarie finds the precious bags right where Timo said she would. Extraordinary. He hasn't worked here in ages, yet he knows exactly where to find stuff. "Thanks, Timo," she says waving a handful of bags. No need to be churlish.

John comes upstairs. "Mo! How ya doin', buddy?" They hug.

"I'm good. You?"

"Can't complain. We sure miss you around here."

"Yeah, I heard about that crazy Newf. Guess you need some help, eh?" Timo is aware of why he's been summoned.

"Randy's from Nova Scotia, actually. He'll be heading home with the wife and kids soon, so I'll be short-handed for a while."

John looks at Timo with hope.

"How's Lina?" Timo asks.

"Not too bad," John replies. "I think she just needs a rest. She keeps forgetting stuff and this morning she called me 'Giuseppe.'"

"Well, you do look a bit like the old man, but all you Falcones look alike. Hope it's not one of them Oedipus things."

"Very funny, Mo. Maybe you shoulda been a psychiatrist instead of a butcher."

Rosemarie counts out ten bags and stuffs the others back where she found them. She's walking away when John says, "Mo, you remember Rose? From high school?"

"Who could forget Rosemarie Catanzaro? The only blonde Italian I ever met. Thought she was one of ours; suoamalainen playing for the wrong team. We just said hello."

John and Timo have been best friends since high school. Rosemarie has known John since kindergarten. When she was little, the kids on Rosemarie's block used to have these epic skipping sessions that would go on until their mothers called them in for supper. Double Dutch was her favourite and while they skipped, they sang made-up jingles to keep the rhythm. The Name Game they called it.

Rosie Catanzaro
wants a Camaro
but her old man drives a Ford.

They had one for John, too:

Johnny Falcone
is full of baloney
but he only eats hot dogs.

They didn't have one for Timo. Rosemarie didn't meet him until she went to high school. Timo was a country kid and rode the school bus with all the other Finlanders from Lappe. Anyhow, they wouldn't have been able to pronounce his last name, let alone find anything to rhyme with Kainulainen.

The three of them were in first-period geography class together. Rosemarie remembers Mr. House teaching the class about the arctic watershed. John and Timo told him they didn't give a hoot what went on beyond Ignace. "Who cares?" they'd said. They weren't going anywhere. Lots of giggles from the class, Ignace being only two and a half hours west of Thunder Bay. Grade nine, day one, and they each knew their own futures. *Well, Rosamarina, they were right! So, while you can name every country in Europe, all the islands of the West Indies, most of the countries in Africa (some by their former colonial names), you've never left the province. Does anyone care that Burkina Faso used to be called Upper Volta? Useless information. Now who's laughing?*

"Rose is gonna help us out for a while," John tells Timo. "You still good at math, Rose? Think you could give me a hand with the payroll?" he asks. "Just till my mom's feeling better."

"Sure, John, I guess I could, but I better get those chickens bagged first."

"Thanks, hon. I'll be in my office. Come down and see me when Tracey comes in. "Buy you a cup of joe, Mo?"

"Why not? See ya, Rose."

"Nice to see you again, Timo," Rosemarie says and hurries off to bag the birds.

Tracey arrives just before noon. Rosemarie notices the tip of her right index finger is bandaged and wrapped in a finger-condom to protect it. Rosemarie asks Tracey how she's doing. Tracey just shrugs. She's quite a bit older than Rosemarie and built like a roller derby queen. Some guys might call her a tough broad.

"Christ, I hate coming in on short notice. I wasn't supposed to be here until tomorrow evening. John caught me off guard when he called. I had a bunch of errands to do that won't get done 'cause I was off yesterday, and now today is shot."

Rosemarie realises that Tracey must need the money and can't afford to stay home. Her apron looks like it could use a wash, same goes for her *Falcone* cap. And although Tracey is not a bad looking woman, she looks haggard and kind of worn out. Who wouldn't after working a few years in this place?

"At least I'll get a decent cheque this week. I was scheduled for forty hours, before *this!*" Tracey says, extending her right index finger into the air. "God knows I could use the OT."

Tracey shoves her purse under the counter where Carol stashes hers. Rosemarie assumes they don't want to leave their valuables unattended in the staff room. Perhaps it could be an invitation to a thief, or maybe, like Carol, Tracey wants to keep her bag handy so she can grab a cigarette whenever there's a lull in the action. Rosemarie hopes that Tracey doesn't smoke, or at least won't take as many smoke breaks. Rosemarie doesn't bring her purse to work. She doesn't want it to smell like an abattoir. Besides that, she's ashamed to admit that she wouldn't want them to see her Coach bag, or worse, the Dooney and Burke.

"Have you been working here long, Tracey?" Rosemarie asks.

Tracey doesn't answer. She glances at Carol with a quizzical look on her face.

Carol nods toward Rosemarie and tells Tracey, "She's a friend of John's."

Rosemarie has no idea why being John's friend would raise an eyebrow, yet that is the effect, although nothing more is said. Rosemarie grabs a bun from the bakery display in the front of the store and makes herself a sandwich. She tells Carol she's going to take her break.

"Get Gord to bring up a roll of butcher paper if you see him," Carol says.

"I can bring one when I come back if you tell me where to find it," Rosemarie volunteers. Again, Carol and Tracey exchange puzzling glances.

"It's too heavy for you," Carol says.

Rosemarie realises they don't want her to do anything that the other women don't want to do. When Rosemarie went to the freezer to fetch a case of ribs the other day, Carol told her she should have got one of the guys to help her. Rosemarie told Carol that she likes to at least *target* equality. Rosemarie reckons she stands alone on that issue.

The stairwell is filled with stock waiting to go downstairs to the storeroom. A conveyor belt runs alongside the stairway. Two large buttons—one red, one green, control its operation.

The first time Rosemarie used the conveyor she learned a valuable lesson. She was sent downstairs to collect gallon-size jars of marinated mushrooms and sun-dried tomatoes to refill the olive bar. Gord saw Rosemarie struggling and handed her an empty milk crate.

He told Rosemarie to use the conveyor. She placed the heavy crate on the belt at the bottom of the stairs and pushed the green button. *Well, that's curious,* Rosemarie thought, rather than *ascending* to the main floor, the belt was going the wrong way! Gord leapt into action. Like a superhero, he shoved Rosemarie out of the way and caught the crate before it fell on the floor, preventing a painful, not to mention *costly,* accident. Gord hit the stop button and reversed the mechanism before Rosemarie knew what was happening.

Rosemarie is cautious as she steps over the incoming stock. She spots Gord and watches him empty the contents of a metal box into the garbage. "What is that thing?" she asks.

"This," Gord says, tightening a spring-loaded knob on the side of the contraption, "is the Hotel California." Gord sets it down on the floor against one wall. "Basically, it's a deluxe mousetrap." He quotes a line from the Eagles, "*... you can check out anytime you like, but you can never leeeeeave.*" Once Gord squeals out the guitar riff, Rosemarie asks him where she might find a roll of butcher paper. Gord offers to get it when he's free. Rosemarie doesn't argue. They've got Gord well-trained and surely one superhero is enough for any deli. Rosemarie hops over a pile of boxes and heads downstairs, glad she didn't meet any "hotel guests."

The storeroom is stocked to the rafters with cases of expensive imported food products arranged on shelves that surround the walk-in cooler, where deli items and produce are stored. It's a scavenger hunt to find anything inside the cooler. The store's policy of first-in, first-out requires enough space to rotate the stock to avoid spoilage. However, Rosemarie often spends a lot of extra time in search of an item she needs because, rather than take the time to put things where they're supposed to, her co-workers have buried it behind incoming stock.

The walk-in freezer, where Rosemarie has occasionally ventured to look for a whole case of chicken breasts or burger patties for a customer buying in bulk, is even worse. It's treacherously overloaded beyond capacity, with a total lack of organization. Every moment inside becomes urgent due to the sub-zero temperature.

A prep area is located opposite the walk-in cooler. It's equipped with a hand-wash station, a meat grinder used exclusively for making the famous sausage, and a "slow cook 'n hold" oven that's in constant use roasting meat for the daily lunch menu. Every Wednesday they serve Italian sausage on a bun; Thursdays are devoted to Southern-style pulled pork; Fridays are hot roast beef on a bun and they also sell take-away containers filled with beef au jus. On weekends, special orders for parties fill every available space on the stainless steel counters which is also where they make pre-packaged salads sold in the self-serve coolers. A large three-compartment sink is fitted with a high-pressure sprayer to hose down the entire area.

In the farthest corner of this maze is a lunchroom where staff can take a quick break and post notes to one another regarding the swapping of shifts and booking of holidays. It is always in a despicable state of disarray. Newspapers, shoes, aprons, caps, jackets, and a motley collection of deserted personal belongings clutter the small windowless room. A basket of assorted items, mostly olive oil and salad dressings that have surpassed their sell-before-date, are left for the staff to rummage through and take home at no cost. In the opposite corner of the basement, beyond the staff washrooms, Rosemarie spots rolls of butcher paper in two different sizes and cases of custom-printed "Falcone" butcher tape stacked near the bottom of another stairwell that leads up to the cashiers stations in the front of the store. Under that stairwell, in the very bowels of this enterprise, is the office where John waits for Rosemarie.

She taps on the open door and says, "Hi, John. Is this a good time?"

"Come on in, Rose. Here, you can sit at Lina's desk." John pulls out a chair for Rosemarie and clears away a two-foot stack of papers. "It's kind of a mess since my mom's been off." John reaches into the safe, pulls out a handful of time cards and says, "We have to figure out Vacation Pay since this will be Randy's last pay cheque. Same with Tiffany. I think there's a book of deduction tables around here somewhere, let me see... here it is."

Rosemarie is shocked. "You mean to tell me you do this manually? You're not computerized?" Astonishing, considering it's the twenty-first century and there's a computer sitting on the desk.

"My mom hates computers, and to tell you the truth, I never really use this one." John looks embarrassed. He holds up his index finger and says, "Hunt and peck, you know? It's a lot easier for me to use the phone instead of spending all morning typing an e-mail."

"Oh. Okay," Rosemarie says. "What about severance pay?"

"They both quit. Far as I know, I don't have to pay severance," John says.

"That's right. Not if they quit." Rosemarie should know, she didn't get a nickel from the board of education. Rosemarie assumes John gave Randy and Tiffany the option to resign, not to save the two-weeks severance pay, more likely to do them a favour and keep a dismissal off their permanent records. He really is a nice guy.

"Okay, John. Mind if I eat my lunch while I take a look at these? Are these all the time cards?"

"Yeah, I think so. I mean, yes, you go right ahead and enjoy your lunch first. Is that porchetta? Good choice, Rose. I think these are all the time cards, but we only need to pay Randy and Tiffany right away. Payday isn't till Monday. Normally, my mom does the payroll when she comes in Sunday evenings to do the schedule. I'm gonna go up and help with the orders. I'll be back shortly. Here's the cheque book. I can sign them when you're done. Call me if you need anything. And thanks a million, Rose. You're a lifesaver."

Rosemarie finds time cards for the two recently departed lovebirds. The first thing she discovers is that Tiffany, who had been working here for a couple of years, wasn't making much more than Rosemarie is. The second thing Rosemarie notices is how much money a meat cutter makes! Perhaps she should reconsider her future and brush up on her knife skills. Rosemarie calculates their respective hours, adds 4% for vacation pay, finds the corresponding tax, EI and CPP deductions in the antiquated Canada Revenue *Tables for Deductions at Source*, and issues two pay cheques. A cinch.

John comes back before Rosemarie can sneak a look at the other time cards. "How ya makin' out, Rose?"

"Good. Here's the cheques. Do you want to take a look at the cheque register, John?"

"No, that's okay, Rose. I trust you," John says and signs the cheques. "I better get back to work."

"What about ROE's?"

"English please, Rose."

"Record of Employment. You have to file one with Service

Canada when an employee leaves."

"Oh. Thanks for reminding me. I'll check with Lina, but I gotta get back to work right now. Short-handed, you know. We'll talk later. I'll leave these with the cashiers," John says. He waves the cheques and dashes off.

Rosemarie takes a few extra minutes to freshen up in the ladies' room before she returns to work. She pauses in the receiving area to take a look at next week's schedule which should be up by now.

Rosemarie is annoyed that she forgot to bring her Day-Timer with her to record her shifts. Then she remembers she pitched it out because there were so many appointments she would not be keeping. Instead, Rosemarie culls a scrap of paper from the garbage bin to jot down her next shift.

The schedule for next week still hasn't been posted. Rosemarie hasn't figured out the scheduling system yet (assuming there is one!). She's not scheduled to work this weekend but without knowing what her hours will be next week, it's difficult to plan anything in advance. So far, Rosemarie's shifts have been all over the clock, switching back and forth between days and evenings while she's in training and filling in for Angie, who is on vacation. It occurs to Rosemarie that without Tiffany, the schedule will need to be changed. She takes a closer look and sees that somebody scribbled Rosemarie's name in over Tiffany's two-close shift on Sunday. *Shit.* Rosemarie doesn't mind working the odd evening shift; it's usually less stressful than days, but Sundays are the worst. They have to clean the meat cases and don't get finished until very late at night. And Sunday afternoon in the dying days of summer is the busiest time slot of the whole week, so Rosemarie knows she'll be exhausted and miss dinner at her mom's, again.

John kicks open the cutting-room door and throws an empty box on the pile of cardboard that has accumulated beside the time-clock in the receiving area.

"Sorry, Rose, didn't see you there. I penciled you in to cover Tiffany's shift on Sunday. Hope that doesn't mess up your plans for the weekend."

"Actually, John, it does kind of mess things up for me. Not because I have plans, which I do, I mean... have plans." *Oh for chrissakes, just tell him.* "I really don't like to work the closing-shift, especially when we have to clean the meat cases. I think I'm just too old for this kind of work."

"Oh don't say that. You're not old, Rosie. And you're doing great!"

"I don't mean it like that. It's just... working with these young guys, you know, they kind of... oh, never mind."

"I hear you, Rose. Those young fellas can be very annoying. But this weekend we're gonna be real busy, and without Tiffany, we sure could use your help."

"Well, I suppose if I didn't have to come in quite so early I could handle it. But two-to-close is just too hard for me," Rosemarie says, surprised now at her own nerve.

"Here, tell you what." John pulls the schedule down off the wall. "Can you make it in by four?"

"I guess I could this time, but I really don't want to work any more evenings, John. If you need me to help out on day shift till Angie comes back, no problem. But I think I'll have to look for something else."

John scribbles out two-close and changes it to four-close. "I don't want to lose you, Rose. You tell me what shifts you don't want and I'll fix it."

"Last week I worked two closing-shifts and was scheduled in early the following mornings. Then I spent my day off unable to do anything because I was so tired."

"No, you're right. That's not fair." John rifles through the schedule and sees that the other pages are all from weeks ago. He looks disappointed and a little embarrassed.

"The schedule for next week isn't up yet," Rosemarie tells him.

"I've been kind of busy with my own stuff lately," John confesses. "I never noticed what was going on. My mom usually makes the schedule. She's supposed to do at least three weeks ahead."

"Is she sick?" Rosemarie asks.

"Well, yeah, sort of. Maybe I can muddle through it. I'll try to have it for Sunday when you come in."

"Meat Department, line one... "

"Sorry, Rose, I gotta grab the phone. Hang in there. I'll fix it. I promise."

Rosemarie is mad at herself for being such a pushover. Why didn't she just say no? He's just so goddamn *nice*. She strides through the deli, grabs a pair of gloves and hurries over to the hand sink. Carol pounces.

"It's about time!" Carol is annoyed with Rosemarie for taking what she thinks was an extra long break.

"Sorry, Carol, I should have–"

"You've been gone for ages. We thought you ran off or something," Carol yells. "I'm going for a smoke. The counter needs filling," she declares, and before Rosemarie can explain, Carol is gone.

What a day. It felt like six o'clock would never come. Even if she had a chance, Rosemarie didn't have the nerve to take her second break and risk another dressing down from Carol. And by the time Tracey took her break, they were already into the dinner rush.

Rosemarie picks up a hand basket and purchases a few groceries. She heads across Connie Street to where she parked in the designated staff-parking lot.

Rosemarie doesn't need to drive to work. Her apartment is only a couple of blocks away and the long summer evenings are still warm enough that she might enjoy the walk home if her feet weren't so goddamn sore. *Better get used to it.* Rosemarie climbs into her car and revs the engine for the short trip home.

Lina's Assessment

"So, Lina's not crazy?" John listens intently. He still can't quite follow what the doctor is trying to explain.

"We don't say crazy, Mr. Falcone," the specialist explains with restrained hostility. "Most schizophrenics respond very well to the drugs. Since your mother's condition continues to degrade, we would normally consider changing the medication, but there's a weaning period that will take longer than our assessment period allows for. Perhaps she just needs a little more time. Every patient responds differently. I don't know what else to tell you, Mr. Falcone. I've only ever seen this sort of behaviour when a patient goes *off* their meds."

"I wish you'd quit calling me that, Doc. Makes me feel old. How do you know for sure she's taking the medication?" John asks.

"We have procedures in place, Mr. Falcone, to ensure that the medication is administered according to strict protocol."

"Lina can be quite a trickster," John says.

"Indeed, that's the schizophrenic's specialty, if you will."

"Well, she's not your average schizo," John argues in Lina's defence. "But then she's the only one I know. Are you sure it's not dementia or what's it? Alzheimer's? She's never been this bad before, just kind of forgetful."

"Quite. Certainly her memory problems are a factor, but your mother is exhibiting many other signs not typically associated with dementia. Delusions, hallucinations even, all classic symptoms of schizophrenia. Combined with disorganized behaviour, thought disorder and her lack of interest in everyday activities, I believe my diagnosis to be correct, Mr. Falcone. That's why I had her moved from the interim care facility. We'll be able to monitor her behaviour better from our psych ward."

John looks a bit dazed and confused himself. "She's never been interested in anything outside of work," he says. "She's always had difficulty paying attention, and I never know when she's gonna blow a gasket—what you wanna call *disorganized behaviour*, but she's usually under a lot of stress. And to tell you the truth, Doc, I'm not surprised she's not interested in socializing. I mean, no offence, but it's pretty dull around here, eh?"

"It's Bond. Doctor Bond. And as I said, these are all classic symptoms which she could have been displaying for many years. Certainly stressful life circumstances combined with her age may have contributed to the acceleration of the disease, but for now I'm ruling out other psychotic disorders."

"You're the expert," John says. "I'll talk to her and make sure she follows your orders."

"Excellent. We rely on the family's support at a crucial time like this. For now we will have to continue to keep her confined and monitored. If you feel she could be better stimulated by outside visitors, I encourage you to have them stop in for short visits. Too often the stigma of mental health issues keeps people from getting involved. Thank you for coming in, Mr. Falcone. My receptionist will see that you receive a copy of my report."

Rosemarie climbs the flight of stairs to her second floor apartment and feels like she's ascending the CN Tower. She drops her bag of groceries on the top step and pulls at her shoes without bending over to untie them. The message light is blinking on her phone and Rosemarie stumbles, rushing to see if Brian has called. One message from her best friend Jen, and two missed calls from her mother. She hasn't talked to Jen since she lost her job and Jen sounds a bit frantic. First things first.

"Hi, mom. It's me. How are you?"

"Who?" Rosemarie's mother aks, egging her on.

Rosemarie gives it right back. "Your long-lost daughter. The good-for-nothing unmarried childless one."

"Oh, it's you, Rosamarina! I didn't recognize your voice." *As if "Hi, mom," wasn't a clue.*

"I just got home from work, and I'm wiped out. And before you ask, I can't come for dinner on Sunday. I have to work."

"Rosamarina! Your sister and the girls will be so disappointed. We haven't seen you in weeks. Why don't you just tell that Johnny

Falcone that you don't work on the Sabbath."

"It's our busiest day, Ma. And please, don't even go there," she implores. "Say hi to Roseanna and the girls and tell them I'll stop by as soon as I have some time."

"Oh, sure. I'll do your dirty work." *My mother, the martyr.* "I'm making *bagna cauda*, so long as the peppers come in." *Passive aggressive, too.*

Rosemarie loves that stuff. Her mother's secret weapon is *bagna cauda*; delicious roasted red peppers swimming in garlicky butter and olive oil, sauteed so slowly the garlic turns to a nutty sweet mush. Rosemarie always regrets the quantity of fresh bread she consumes to soak up every last morsel. She spends the rest of the week sweating out a jillion calories at the gym. She might as well get a trowel and apply it directly to her hips.

Her mother's people are from northern Italy–Lombardia and Piedmont–where the regional cooking is very different than that of Calabria, where her father's family (and half of Port Arthur) came from. Rosemarie inherited her mother's fair complexion and light hair colour, while Rosemarie's sister Rosanna takes after their father and has the classic dark look of a Southerner. Their dad used to tell them he got one of each, equal but different, although Rosemarie always thought he liked her sister best. Both of the girls inherited their mother's sassy attitude. Unfortunately, neither of them have had the time to study their mom's culinary skills. She does fantastic things with veal and mushrooms, and her risotto is beyond comparison.

"I'll be there next Sunday for sure, Ma. Cross my heart."

"*Dio nini!* You better," her mother warns and hangs up.

Rosemarie unpacks her groceries. She's always loved to shop at Falcone, and with her staff discount, she can still splurge a little. For dinner she bought a filet of wild sockeye salmon that came in this morning. It looked so fresh she snapped it up before it sold out. She also picked up a bag of new potatoes, a head of leaf lettuce and a pint of fresh local strawberries. She even scored a free bottle of Paul Newman's Italian dressing from the grab basket in the staff lunchroom. She can nuke the potatoes and toss a salad while the fish cooks. Rosemarie pours a glass of wine from the open bottle of Chianti she's been working on for a couple of days and heads upstairs.

A winding oak staircase leads to the rooftop sunroom that overlooks the marina and harbour at the head of Lake Superior. Light pours in through the wall to wall windows that face the lake and rise at a dramatic angle from the floor to the high, vaulted ceiling. A narrow piano window set in the south wall over the stairwell allows a glimpse of Mount McKay in the distance. Opposite the lake view, two smaller arched windows form a frame for the glass garden-door that faces west. It's fitted with a whimsical screen door that opens onto the deck.

Rosemarie's apartment is a masterpiece of modern convenience. Of course she's paying ransom for it and she's probably going to lose it when she can't make the next payment. Luckily, the rent is controlled and can only be increased by the annual change to the Consumer Price Index. If she were to consider taking in a roommate, Rosemarie thinks she just might be able to hang onto it. Finding someone willing to share the rent should be easy considering its assets: centrally located downtown with open-concept living, dining and kitchen area equipped with commercial cooking appliances. Two bedrooms, two bathrooms, self-contained laundry room. The master bedroom is huge, with more closets than Rosemarie has skeletons. The en suite is kitted out with old-fashioned porcelain fixtures and a Jacuzzi. Hardwood flooring covers the main floor located above the old warehouse, now occupied by an off-site data storage company. They're great neighbours, providing sterling security. They've armed the building with the latest technology and only have a couple of employees who are seldom seen or heard. Anyone with discerning taste would want to live here if only it wasn't smack-dab in the middle of the scruffiest neighbourhood in town.

On one side of Superior Street, Rosemarie's neighbours live in a transition residence for the not-too-mentally-ill. On the other side there's a drug dealer. Directly across the street is an escort service with taxis coming and going at all hours of the night, delivering the *working girls* to and from their "dates." There used to be quite a few whore houses in this neighbourhood, but after the City cleaned up Simpson Street and the Casino opened, the street-walkers moved in and the madams sold out to drug dealers and their *pets*. Ferocious pit bull terriers are a gangster's best friend. Whenever the cops try to bust a dealer, he invariably tells them to hang on while he ties up his vicious guard dog–trained to scare the daylights out of any unexpected visitors. This gives him plenty of time to dispose of or hide his stash while the terrified crime-fighters wait on the porch. Even the dog catcher comes with backup.

A handful of rooming houses flesh out the rest of the block, their residents mostly alcoholics and impoverished natives. Scattered between are a few seedy bars, a Chinese take-out that does an excellent hot 'n sour soup, a couple of recently-opened upscale restaurants, a used-car dealer, The Northern Woman's Bookstore, and, according to Rosemarie's Canada Post letter carrier, more beauty salons per capita than anywhere else in Thunder Bay, possibly the country. The same could be said of hookers and drug dealers but their mail isn't likely addressed to *"Whore to Door Escort Service"* or *"Jack's Crack Emporium."* When Rosemarie was a kid, the neighbourhood was famous for its house of ill repute run by a flamboyant madam, who was often in the news. The City expropriated most of the land under the guise of urban renewal and the area has undergone many changes since the madam died.

The entire area is under transformation. Just one block south of this matrix a new hotel and luxury condos are going to be constructed at the marina. Once complete, Rosemarie's address is destined to become desirable.

The building itself is not a very old one but it has its place in the history of Port Arthur. It was built in the 50's by RF Welsh Construction, a contracting company that brought immigrants from Calabria to work on the CN road gangs. Rosemarie's dad worked here.

The twin cities of Port Arthur and Fort William were amalgamated in 1970. Rosemarie remembers hearing about the famous referendum with the split vote. In their infinite wisdom, the founding fathers put three choices on the ballot to name the new city: Lakehead, *The* Lakehead, and Thunder Bay. Lots of people still refer to Thunder Bay as the Lakehead, but only the diehards call the north side of the city "Port Arthur," and the south side, "Fort

William." Although Rosemarie was born a decade after the amalgamation, she was raised by parents who fell into the "diehard" category. Rosemarie isn't against using the city's correct name. She's fascinated by the controversy and she likes the way the old names sound. It reminds her of the way the neighbourhoods of Toronto all have their own special vibe. Cabbage Town, The Beaches, The Danforth... insiders know they're in Toronto but would never use the word to describe where they live.

Stepping out onto the deck affords an outside look at the sunroom that was added onto the building in the 80's after RF Welsh sold out. Clad in pink siding, decorated with wooden shutters and a dash of gingerbread trim it looks like a crazy playhouse that landed on the roof, Kansas style. The cedar deck is enclosed behind a six-foot-high wooden fence on three sides, and by the sunroom that blocks the cold breeze blowing in off the big lake they call Gitchigoomi. If she's up early enough and stays up late enough, Rosemarie can see the sun rise over the Sleeping Giant and watch it set over Hillcrest Park.

Rosemarie lights the barbecue and flops down into her deck chair. She looks around at the dreadful condition of the herb garden and flower beds. The heat of the midsummer evening is intense. The flowers will only wilt if Rosemarie waters the plants before it cools down a little. Her namesake is in need of a drink as much as she is. So are the roses, which are nothing but heartache and crawling with aphids. And the over-ripe blackberries have been ravaged by birds. *Shit!* Rosemarie was waiting for those to ripen so she could do a crème framboise. Last year she only got a handful of berries but they were so delicious she decided to do something special with them.

Even Brian, who never likes anything "weird," thought it was the best thing he'd ever tasted. Rosemarie gets up and gorges herself on the birds' leftovers. To hell with the pud! Who needs the calories?

Rosemarie can barely hear what goes on down at street level, the voices are drowned out by white noise produced by the garden's water feature. It's nothing more than an old watering can and a galvanized basin filled with river stones, but it has a soothing effect, and she fights to stay awake.

As soon as the barbecue is hot enough, Rosemarie throws the salmon fillet on the grill skin side down, gives it a squirt of lemon juice, and closes the lid. Rosemarie finds this the easiest way to cook salmon. Clean-up is simplified by sliding the fish onto the plate when it's done, leaving the skin stuck to the grill until it burns to a crisp. The trick is to remember to remove the skin from the grill once it's cool or Rosemarie will have to clean up after seagulls attracted by the fishy smell and listen to their incessant cries of, "Feed me! Feed me!"

The fish cooks quickly and Rosemarie polishes off the cheap red wine with her feast. Red wine with fish? *No rules, when you drink alone. Cheers!*

While the tub fills, Rosemarie rinses her dishes and notices her shoes laying in the middle of the floor where she yanked them off. The treads are full of meat product. *Yuk!* She kicks them down the stairs and vows to start leaving them at work.

Rosemarie strips off her clothes, tosses them directly into the washing machine, and trundles off to the Jacuzzi for the same treatment. She could drown in there if she's not careful, yet the warm lavender-scented water revives her long enough to water the garden when she's finished soaking. The roses and the rosemary show their gratitude with a heavenly scented whiff.

Summer is waning. The sun has dipped below the horizon, casting a golden-pink glow over the rooftops. Rosemarie crawls into bed filled with a lightness bordering on euphoria. She doesn't want to move. She's connected to this place. Her dad died here.

Rosemarie wakes up staring at the clock with mild alarm until she realises she doesn't have to be at work this morning. She forces herself out of bed to make coffee. She skips breakfast and dresses in a pair of shorts and a tank top. Rosemarie rummages through her closet, ignoring the impressive shoe collection she amassed over several years while she was earning a substantial income. She finds her old Birkenstocks, grabs her purse and keys and braces herself for the stressful confrontation that is inevitable.

Rosemarie runs down the stairs and before she can jump into her car, she meets the letter carrier who hands her a stack of window-envelopes. Rosemarie tosses them into the mailbox without another glance. She knows they are bills.

With the turn of a key everything changes. Her stress evaporates. The purr of the engine is as soothing as a chamber orchestra and the feel of the Alfa Romeo's palomino leather on her bare legs is... *Oh, God. Stop that.* The car glides out onto the street and Rosemarie is transported in more ways than one. No matter the destination, the drive is always too short. In just a few minutes she finds herself parked in front of the dealership, its ersatz architecture a towering marvel of glass and steel on a budget.

When Rosemarie enters the showroom, it appears to be deserted. She calls out, "Hello?" and instantly, salesmen scurry out from wherever they've been hiding, like cockroaches.

"Well, hello there," one of the smarmy salesmen says.

"Something I can show you this morning?" an even more oleaginous one asks.

"I'd like to see the finance manager, please."

"Let me see if François is available. Would you like coffee? We have espresso or cappuccino."

"No, thanks. I'm kind of in a hurry."

"I'll go see if I can find him." The sales rep disappears behind one of the many doors.

He's back in a moment and says, "François is on a conference call. We have herbal tea if you prefer. Help yourself. He'll be with you in a jiffy."

Before Rosemarie can sit down, the finance manager glides toward her, hand extended, 100-watt smile screwed on.

"Well, good morning, Ms. Catanzaro," he oozes. *How does he remember my name?* "Come to see this year's model, or are you still in love with the Spider's incredible design and engineering?" he purrs, not unlike her car.

"Actually, I need to talk to you about the lease terms," Rosemarie says.

"Please, come into my office. Let me pull your file." François leaves Rosemarie staring at the awards he's garnered, gracing the walls of his cubicle like a doctor's surgery. *How long could he possibly have been at this? Two, maybe three years, max. He doesn't look old enough to shave.*

He's back, holding a slim manilla folder and frowning. "I see you've taken the extended 48-month plan, did you want to increase your payments and take a shorter term? Good move with interest rates so low, and if you can swing it, you'll reach your buy-out option sooner."

"No. I was hoping to *lower* the payments and *extend* the terms."

François sits with his elbows on his desk. He holds his fingers together doing the church/steeple thing, while he pretends to ponder the issue. "I'm afraid that's not possible, ma'am."

What happened to Ms?

"You could consider taking the buy-out now, although it will cost a little more up front, you'll actually save a bit of interest."

With no attempt to disguise her hostility, through gritted teeth Rosemarie spits, "If I had the money for a buy-out, I wouldn't be asking you to lower the payments, would I? I'm between jobs and my insurance is due at the end of the month. I can't afford to make the payments right now."

"I see. Perhaps a friend or relative could extend a loan?" François suggests.

"Impossible," Rosemarie says flatly. "Is Bernard, here? Maybe he can help?" Rosemarie used to work for Bernard when he owned the McTavish Hotel. She started out as a banquet waitress while she went to university. After graduating, Rosemarie worked her way up to the accounting office and eventually took over "personnel" as it was known back then. "Surely there's something he can do."

"I'm afraid Bernard is abroad, but I can assure you, he won't be able to facilitate anything that I can't handle for you. Finance is *my* department."

Rosemarie is getting nowhere fast and starts to feel a little dizzy.

"Have you thought about a trade-in on something a little more... *affordable*? We just got a little gem in yesterday. Toyota Corolla, nice little car for around town, low mileage and a steal at–"

Rosemarie's lower lip starts to quiver.

"... let's see, what sort of monthly payment would you be comfortable with?"

Rosemarie's mom has been driving that same model for more than a decade and would gladly let her borrow it anytime, but she never wanted to be seen in that rust bucket. Rosemarie is gonna lose it. She has to get out of there. *Now!*

Rosemarie drops the keys on the desk and makes a dash for the door. François is right behind her, imploring Rosemarie to wait until he can sort out the paper work. She's out of the showroom before he can catch her.

Rosemarie runs across Memorial Avenue without looking. The pounding of her heart is deafening. She doesn't hear the screeching tires of a transport truck that stops within an inch of her so-called life. She catches her breath and chokes back hot tears, flowing now like the Kam River in spring. Rosemarie slows down to a brisk pace and doesn't stop until she's in front of the main entrance to Service Canada. She ransacks her purse looking for a Kleenex while government employees out for their smoke break try to pretend they don't notice her. Rosemarie glares at them and blows her nose.

Inside, Rosemarie is told that her employment councillor is off until Monday. She takes a peek at the job-postings and sees nothing has changed since the last time she was here and probably won't anytime soon. Not before the rent is due. Recognizing that this is a total waste of her time, Rosemarie sets out for the long walk home.

A thunder storm is brewing. Rosemarie sees a bank of taxis lined up in front of the Superstore. She climbs into the back seat of a cab as the first fat drops hit the windshield. "Where to?" asks the driver.

"Superior Street, between Court and Cumberland."

When they get to Rosemarie's block the cab driver turns off the metre and cranks his head around to get a better look at her. The metre shows $9.80. "On the house account?" he inquires.

"Here." Rosemarie pushes a ten into the driver's hand. "Keep the change," she says sarcastically. For a moment, Rosemarie regrets that she's not the working girl the cabbie thinks she is. *Wonder what an escort makes?* The only answer Rosemarie can come up with is; *a lot more than me! And they don't need a car.*

Back upstairs in her sanctuary, Rosemarie calms herself with a cup of mint tea and a bowl of strawberries. She remembers she hasn't called Jen back yet and decides to get it over with.

"Hey, Girlfriend."

"Oh, my God! Where have you been? I've tried your cell about a million times and keep getting this weird message. And you're never home. What's going on, Cat?"

Cat. Short for Catanzaro. Rosemarie has been stuck with that one since grade five. The boys had a ball with it in grade nine. *Here pussy, pussy....*

"Sorry, Jen, I haven't had a chance to tell you about my crappy luck. And I had to give my Blackberry back when I quit."

"Quit?" Jen yelps. "What were you thinking?

"I didn't want to quit, the board forced me to. You must have heard about the incident. It was on the news."

"That thing with the kid's haircut? They fired you for that?"

"No. I told you, I quit. I wanted to fire the Teacher's Assistant. The board didn't want to take on the union, so I was the fall gal."

"That's not fair!" Jen whines. "I heard that kid was growing his hair out for a pow-wow or something. Didn't they say he couldn't see the blackboard?"

"Yeah. But the TA could have called his mother and told her that. She didn't have to take a pair of scissors to him. Native kids are very sensitive to that sort of thing. It's part of their culture. You don't touch them, especially their hair. They say it's connected to the person's spirit."

"Wow. How do you know all that?"

"I lost my job over it, Jen!"

Rosemarie shocked herself when she took a stand on an issue she knew so little about. At the time, her gut reaction was that it was wrong for the teacher's assistant to do it, but Rosemarie had no idea what a big deal it was going to be until the media got a hold of the story.

"So what are you going to do now?" Jen asks.

"I'm looking for another job and working at Falcone in the meantime," Rosemarie confesses.

"Falcone! Jeez, Cat, you're full of surprises. I suppose Brian is jealous that you're hanging around that babe, Johnny Falcone. Are they hiring? Can you get me in there? As Johnny's personal masseuse, maybe?"

"Brian went with the Blackberry. You think John's hot?"

"Duh. Yeah! What do you mean, Brian's gone? Where?"

"I have no idea, sipping cocktails at the Ice Hotel for all I care. We're through. Anyhow, I can't talk, I've got about a million things to do today. I just wanted to let you know I'm alive. I'll call you again when I get a day off."

"Okay, we'll do lunch and you can tell me all about your latest adventure."

"Thanks, Jen, I will. But it's not an adventure, believe me."

Adventure. As if. Jen thinks Rosemarie's life is a lark. And John is hot. How did she not notice that?

Next on Rosemarie's to-do list is laundry. She dumps the hamper onto the floor and starts to sort. Brian's cashmere sweater tumbles out with the rest of the neglected delicates she's been meaning to hand-wash. The salesman called it *fawn* (an expensive shade of beige) and claimed it was combed from the bellies of baby goats raised in the rugged highlands of Mongolia. Its lightweight fleece is as insubstantial as the man she bought it for. Rosemarie buries her face in the deep pile and inhales. It smells like him. Her throat tightens and tears well up again. The heady scent triggers a memory of another expensive gift and just before the dam breaks, Rosemarie recalls that although she likes the smell of *Joop!*, she always thought Brian wore too much cologne. Rosemarie throws the stinking thing on top of the small pile and resolves to let the machine do her dirty work.

While the washer fills, Rosemarie looks around for other signs of Brian. He rarely left his personal belongings behind and only occasionally slept over, usually when he drank too much to drive home. Brian forgot his sweater the last time he spent the night here. He'd shown up late, half-drunk after a golf tournament, and fell asleep almost immediately. They didn't even make love. Rosemarie had left for work before Brian woke up the next morning.

Rosemarie is hungry now and peeks into the fridge. She pitches out a half-loaf of mouldy bread and a bit of cheese that could pass for a science experiment. She discovers a couple of eggs that have been in there so long she's afraid to crack one in case Big Bird pops out. Aside from condiments, there's nothing edible. Rosemarie heads out again with the intent to refill the larder and maybe check the schedule at Falcone.

Out on the street everything smells fresh and clean. The sun has burned off the rain, intensifying the heat with extreme humidity. It's going to be another scorcher. When Rosemarie reaches the store, the parking lot is empty except for a forty-foot trailer backed-up to the loading dock. The lunch rush is over and the day is already half gone.

Rosemarie heads for the produce section and waves at her colleagues behind the meat counter. Frankie shouts, "Rose! What are you doing here on your day off?"

"Just came to pick up a few things."

"The peppers are in," Frankie says. "They're earlier than expected. Better grab some now before you have to fight for them."

"Thanks, Frankie, I will." Rosemarie wanders over to the receiving area where Gord is almost buried in cases of fresh vegetables. Due to the unseasonably hot weather all over Ontario, the tomatoes were early this year, too. For the same reason, the grapes will probably be late. The produce is picked and shipped overnight from the Niagara Peninsula. The trouble is they never know for sure when it's going to arrive until the reefer truck is in transit. Sometimes if they have space in the parking lot, the driver will spot the trailer and come back for it when it's empty. Not only is there no space in Falcone's parking lot, there's no space in the coolers either, so they'll have to sell the peppers immediately.

"Hi, Gord. Can I lighten your load and take a case of peppers before they disappear?"

"Sure thing, Rose. But Lina usually looks after the bulk stuff, so you better check with John because the cashiers won't know what to charge," Gord says. He nods toward the loading dock where John is signing for the shipment.

Rosemarie pauses to take a fresh look at her old friend and new boss. John is handsome, she can't deny that. He's not a big man but he's built for this line of work. The driver throws a case of peppers to John and he catches it easily then tosses it over to Gord. John is stripped down to a T-shirt and Rosemarie notes the rippling biceps, normally hidden under his butchers' smock. "Hey, Rosie! Come to give us a hand?"

Rosemarie is ambushed by a perfect set of straight white teeth that scupper behind John's smile. John pulls off his cap to wipe the sweat from his brow and a wavy lock of mahogany hair spills out. Stylish cut. Smooth olive skin and that brooding look cast by a permanent five o'clock shadow.

"Hi, John. It looks like you have it under control. I'd probably drop the first box you threw at me."

"Two kinds of people in this world, Rosie. At least that's

what my old man always used to say. Catchers and flyers. Trick is to know which one you are!"

"I'm just looking for a case of peppers for my mom. She'll be thrilled to beat the rush!"

"Sure, you go ahead and choose what you want. I'll have to sort out the cost later. It's nice to see you," John adds between catching and releasing, "especially without the Falcone gear. I realise it's not the most flattering uniform for a woman like you."

A woman like me.

"Thanks, John. I only need one case. My mom wants to make *bagna cauda*."

"I love that stuff," John says. "Tell her to save some for me!"

"Sorry, John, not likely. She's doing the peppers on Sunday and she's holding it against you that I won't be there. She probably won't save any for me."

"Really?" John asks in earnest. "I'm sorry, Rose. I didn't mean to cause a problem between you and your mom."

"Don't worry, John. She'll get over it." Rosemarie turns away so John can't see her grinning like an idiot.

"See you Sunday, Rosie!"

Rosemarie opens a case and checks through to make sure there's no rotten peppers hiding in the bottom. They're all ruby red and plump, perfect for roasting. Rosemarie takes the case to the front of the store where she left her shopping basket. She pays for the two bags of groceries and tells the cashier that John said she could take the peppers and settle up later. Gord sees Rosemarie struggling and offers to give her a hand out to her car.

"I walked. I didn't count on buying these," she says, juggling her treasures. "It's only a couple of blocks. I can make two trips."

"If you can hold on a few minutes, I'll give you a lift when I go on deliveries," Gord offers.

"Thanks, Gord. I could use the help today."

Rosemarie returns to the receiving area to check the schedule. Frankie confirms that it hasn't been posted yet.

"You working tomorrow, Rose? I could give you a haircut after work. I need the practice, and no offence, but you could use a trim," Frankie says eying her split-end ponytail with disdain.

"None taken. You're right, I could use a cut but I'm off until Sunday. Want to come over to my place after work tomorrow? I could cook supper," Rosemarie offers in trade.

"Deal."

Rosemarie gives Frankie directions to her place. He promises to bring his scissors and a bottle of wine.

"It's a date, then," Rosemarie says just as Gord comes back jiggling his keys and humming.

"Two-timing me, Rose?" Gord jokes, giving Frankie a playful wink. "Let's roll."

Gord pulls up in front of her building and Rosemarie jumps out. She grabs her stuff and thanks him. Gord speeds off and Rosemarie can hear him singing along with the radio for at least a block.

Rosemarie can't call her mom and ask her to pick up the peppers. She won't come to Rosemarie's apartment. Instead, Rosemarie phones her sister who promises to drop by the next day to collect the peppers on her way to take the girls to soccer practice. Rosemarie's mother has never been to her apartment. *Haunted,* she labelled it, and she may be right. Rosemarie prefers to think of it as "visited upon" from time to time. She feels her father's presence here and welcomes it.

He wasn't exactly killed on the job, but Rosemarie's dad died as a result of injuries sustained while he was replastering the facade. Guido broke his ankle when he tripped over the ladder. Less than three days later a blood clot made its way into his lung and he was gone. *Deep vein thrombosis*, the doctors called it. Rosemarie and her sister were in shock and their mother couldn't believe a 57-year-old man as vital as Guido could die from a broken ankle. According to the nurses, it's a common risk that they're supposed to monitor following surgery. How could they be expected to know Guido would defy orders and try to walk to the bathroom without assistance? Was it their fault he was so stubborn and wouldn't ask for help?

It's not like her father's ghost strolls around the building at night watching over her. Nothing that dramatic. Some people might call him her guardian angel, if they go in for that sort of thing. To Rosemarie, it's more like a good vibe. She has this overwhelming feeling of being protected and that's why she can't bring herself to think about moving. Her dad lives here.

Somewhere a horn toots, nudging Rosemarie out of a deep slumber. The ringing confuses her. More honking catapults Rosemarie from her bed to the phone. "Come on up," she mumbles into the receiver then punches in the code to open the door for her sister, Roseanna.

Rosemarie pads to the kitchen. According to the clock on the wall, it's already after ten, which means she has slept more than twelve hours. A gentle breeze coming in through the open windows a floor above, suddenly turns into a powerful gust as the entrance door, one floor below, opens then slams shut. With a wall-shaking rumble the gush of air propels Rosemarie's sister up the stairs like Mary Poppins on a blustery day.

"Jesus, Mare, this place is haunted! Aren't you up yet?" Roseanna hollers.

"I am now," Rosemarie says, rubbing the sleep from her eyes. "And it's a wind tunnel, not spooks."

"Well it scares the shit out of me whatever it is! And I just about broke my neck tripping over your runners."

"I've told you about a million times to close the outside door before you open the inside door but you're always in such a great big hurry. It only ever happens to you."

"Yeah, well, I'm honoured. And I am. In a hurry, I mean. By the way, they stink, the runners, that is. Which reminds me, that's another thing I gotta do today. Both Sam and Jo need new shoes. Amazons, those girls. They both got new sneakers this spring and they've already outgrown them. Sam's feet are already bigger than mine!"

"What are you feeding them?" Rosemarie asks, astonished at how quickly they're turning into women. "Can I try them on?"

"Their old runners? Sure, they never wear them out. And those two are growing in tandem, so Sam's won't fit Jo for more than a week or two, even if she *would* take her sister's hand-me-downs. Jo will borrow Sam's new stuff before Sam gets to wear it, but there's no way she will accept cast-offs. And by the time the other two grow into anything recyclable, it's out of style. And we both know that's a crime against humanity. Anyhow, what's wrong with yours? Other than smelling like a rat's nest, I mean."

"Too tight. If Sam's feet are bigger than yours they should fit me."

"Definitely. Glad to pass them on. Don't tell mom or she'll start calling you *Hand Me Down Rose* again. Where are the peppers? I gotta go. I left the girls in the van."

"Right here. Hang on a sec. I'll get dressed and come down with you."

"Never mind. I'm in a rush and if I don't go right away, they'll kill each other. You can see them later if you stop by to pick up the shoes." Roseanna charges back down the stairs. "And pitch these stinking things out, will ya, Mare? They're disgusting!"

"Don't forget to close the inside–" Another wall-shaking rumble follows in the wake of her big sister.

Rosemarie assumes that her sister might get lonely with Eddie working out of town, but four girls keep Roseanna so busy she doesn't seem to notice her husband is missing. Roseanna has no life of her own, though it appears she likes it that way. Still, Rosemarie is glad her sister came to collect the peppers, because now she won't have to deal with her mother today.

Rosemarie looks forward to Frankie's visit tonight. She thinks about what she'll cook for him while she puts the coffee on. It will be a nice change to have a man over for dinner, although she doesn't harbour any illusions about Frankie. Her *gaydar* tells her it's a waste of time. And she's not often wrong about that. Something chocolate for dessert will be nice, Rosemarie decides. In fact, she's willing to bet Frankie will absolutely love a chocolate fondue! All her girlfriends do. She'll keep it simple: chicken with pasta, a green salad and a knock-out dessert. That'll leave them lots of time to get to know each other.

Following a morning of Olympic-level housework, Rosemarie's apartment is tidy and at least "hotel clean," which is only slightly less sanitary than "hospital clean." After a quick lunch and a shower, Rosemarie preps the fruit for the fondue. She decides to walk over to her sister's for a visit and to try on Sam's shoes. They live a few blocks away behind the Italian Hall. Considering how close they are, it's ridiculous they don't see each other more often, but as their mother always says, *closest to the church, furthest from God.*

It's another beautiful summer day and it looks like everyone in the neighbourhood has left town for the weekend or they're home sleeping it off. Either way, it's a pleasant stroll and Rosemarie reaches her sister's place just as Roseanna pulls into the driveway.

"I just got back from Mom's," Roseanna yells as she unloads bags of stuff from the van and heads around the side of the house to the back door. "She says thanks for the peppers, but she's still pissed you're not coming for dinner on Sunday. Want a drink? You look parched."

"I'd love something frosty cold. Got any Orangina? Where are the girls?"

"Out, thank God. It'll give us a chance to visit." Roseanna disappears inside the house while Rosemarie sinks into a chair on the back porch.

"Here you go. Cheers!" Roseanna hands Rosemarie a tall glass of their favourite sparkling beverage.

Rosemarie can't disguise the look of disappointment on her face.

"They still sell this stuff in those cute little bottles at Falcone I guess." Roseanna pronounces *Falcone* as if it's a disease, lip curl and all.

"Yeah, but it tastes the same," Rosemarie admits. "And one big bottle probably costs the same as a couple of the cute little ones." Roseanna buys Orangina in two-litre bottles at Renco, along with all the other Italian mamas. Everything is *family-size* in this household.

"It's the same price as *one*," Rosemarie's price-savvy sister says, "and speaking of cute, what's it like working for John?"

"It's not all that bad, I guess. Just a lot different than what I used to do." Rosemarie steers the conversation away from that dark place. "Hey, what about Sam's shoes? Did she get a new pair?"

"Oh, yeah. Hang on." Roseanna disappears inside the house for a few minutes. She returns with an armload of sneakers in various sizes and hands a pair to Rosemarie. "These were Sam's. If they're too big, you can try on one of the others. I don't know whose–oh wait... they always put their names inside. These are Jo's."

Rosemarie slips her foot into the first one, and like Cinderella, it's a perfect fit. "Great, now I can go to the ball," she says.

Roseanna laughs. That's the thing with sisters, they always get it. "Prince Charming has lowered his standards," she retorts. That's the other thing with sisters, they know where it hurts.

"Fuck you."

Now they're even.

They sip their Oranginas in silence. After a while Roseanna looks down at her daughter's shoes on her sister's feet and says, "What's going on, Mare?"

"Nothing," Rosemarie lies. "What do you mean?"

"I mean why do you need hand-me-down runners from your niece, is what I mean. Is it that bad?"

"Yeah. Worse." That's all she can manage. After another long pause Rosemarie adds, "Things have kind of spun out of control."

Roseanna stares at her little sister long enough for the silence to become intolerable. When she reaches for Rosemarie's hand, that's all it takes to start the flow of tears.

"Oh, God!" Roseanna whispers, "I had no idea it was that bad. Do you need some money? Eddie will never know the difference and I can tell him I lost it at the casino, which is hardly a lie."

"No way, Zanna. I'll handle it. I'm just stressed out, you

know. I'm fine, really."

"You are not, and you're too fucking stubborn. But the money's here when you need it. You don't have to prove anything, you know. Everybody runs into trouble sometimes," Roseanna says and produces a Kleenex out of thin air.

"I know. But I'm onto something that could turn things around," Rosemarie sniffs. "How do you always know what to say? And where the hell does all the Kleenex come from?"

"Mothers' Union," Roseanna replies, deadpan.

"Well, I gotta get going. Got a man coming for dinner," Rosemarie says in an attempt to lighten things up. She'd like to convince her sister that she's not a complete failure. "And no, it's not Brian," Rosemarie confesses when she sees Roseanna's raised eyebrows. "Thanks for the drink. And the pep talk."

"I mean it, you know, Mare. I can help you out until you get your shit together. No need to start turning tricks," Roseanna jokes.

"Don't knock it. It could add some pizzaz to my résumé. And thank Sam for me, too." Rosemarie picks up the sneakers and leaves before she needs any more Kleenex.

Rosemarie really is onto something. Yesterday, after she left the car dealership in a tizzy, Rosemarie thought about talking to Bernard. Not about her car; she'll have to do without it. She heard a rumour a while ago that Bernard might be involved in the new hotel complex that's going to be built at the marina. The City hasn't awarded the contract yet, but Rosemarie suspects Bernard has put in a tender.

Surely, Bernard will hire her. He's not in tight with any of the school board trustees as far as she knows. That bunch are all capable of holding a grudge like a Hollywood movie producer reeling with indignation. *I'll never work in this town again!* Between them, the school board trustees control the university, the college and the hospital. Bernard could be Rosemarie's ticket back into the private sector.

It would be great to get in on the ground floor of a new hotel and not have to deal with the kind of nightmare they were stuck with at the McTavish when Bernard owned it. When Rosemarie took over HR at the hotel, she was saddled with a stable of lazy, incompetent workers. Waitresses so stubborn and resistant to change they were like a pack of old dogs, virtually untrainable, and so surly the customers were afraid of them. Thieves and drunks in the kitchen, skivers in banqueting, and liars in every department pulling Workers' Comp scams whenever they didn't feel like showing up. Bernard was surrounded by people who would never have been hired in the first place if they hadn't been related to one of the hotel's original four owners. Eventually, Bernard managed to buy out his partners, but he couldn't get rid of the dead weight without triggering an all out war with the union. So Rosemarie had to work with what she had. They did retain a few good employees, and Rosemarie hired some promising new ones when she could. She also put a lot of effort into retraining and things were running smoothly before she left.

Yes, heading up HR and hand-picking employees for a brand new venture would be her dream job, except for one thing—Bernard.

A few minutes past six o'clock, Rosemarie's intercom rings. Before she buzzes Frankie in, Rosemarie tells him to close the entrance door *before* he opens the inside door in the foyer. After her sister's grand entrance this morning, Rosemarie doesn't want to scare Frankie off with talk of spooks. Frankie obeys, and bounds up the stairs carrying a backpack. Rosemarie asks if he remembered to bring his scissors.

"I sure did," Frankie confirms, handing her a bottle of Barolo and pulling a small leather pouch out of his backpack. "I was afraid I might not get out of the store on time so I packed my stuff this morning. I came straight from work. Wow! What a spread! Do I get the nickel tour?"

"Sure, but it'll cost you a dime. Let's grab a drink and I'll show you around. How was work?"

"Shambolic. It's a miracle I got away. The line-up looked threatening but Nick said it was okay to go. He knows they'll wait. How long have you been living here?"

"It'll be three years next month when my lease expires," Rosemarie tells Frankie. She pours two glasses of wine and leads him upstairs to see the deck.

Frankie can't stop asking questions. *"Who built it? When? How can you afford it?"* The usual. Everyone is blown away the first time they see Rosemarie's place. Frankie continues to grill Rosemarie while she grills the chicken.

Frankie agrees that it will be nice to dine *al fresco* so while Rosemarie cooks the pasta, Frankie takes the salad and some plates back up to the deck. He is impressed with the simple dinner and tells Rosemarie she's a good cook.

While Rosemarie and Frankie sit around chatting after dinner, their shadows lengthen in the fading daylight. It's still warm out with a light breeze blowing off the lake. Frankie asks Rosemarie about the circumstances that brought her to his family's business. She tells Frankie about how she lost her job, then her boyfriend and now her car. Rosemarie is tired of dwelling on the subject. She's curious about the big meeting Frankie had with John and Nick last week. When she inquires, Frankie tells Rosemarie about the trouble John is having with Lina.

"John believes his mom is just tired and needs a rest, but me and Nick think it's worse than that. Aunt Lina got so agitated one day, she hit John. That's totally out of character for her, so we convinced John to get her tested for dementia. Nick says it could be early stages of Alzheimer's and with the correct medication she could continue to function pretty well. I'm afraid it's something worse," Frankie says. "She might be cracking up."

Frankie goes on at length. He tells Rosemarie that Lina is currently in St. Joe's Hospital for observation and psychiatric assessment. All three of the Falcone boys are concerned because

Lina's the one who keeps things harmonious. "Sometimes Nick has different ideas about the direction we should take," Frankie says. "Nick doesn't always agree with John, who usually does whatever Lina thinks he should."

"Do either you or Nick have any say in what goes on? At the store, I mean," Rosemarie asks.

"We could, but neither of us are interested in managing the place, although Nick is sort of the manager in the evenings, I guess. Nick likes working nights, and I prefer days," Frankie explains. "We never have the same day off, so the store always has at least one Falcone on site."

"Do you really think Lina is cracking up?"

"I don't know. For some reason she doesn't want me and Nick to visit her," Frankie says. He looks sad when he tells Rosemarie this. "She's the glue. Without her, I don't think we can stick together. And John can't manage the store by himself."

Frankie admits that he doesn't really care about whatever direction the company takes. Given the choice, he says he'd rather do something completely different. He reminds Rosemarie that he always wanted to be a hair stylist. Frankie says he never made it an issue because he feels obliged to his family. "And where would I get the money to study hair design without forcing them to buy me out?" he asks rhetorically.

"Well, I hope they can sort it out. And I hope Lina gets the help she needs," Rosemarie says while she clears away their plates. "I also hope you like chocolate fondue. I've got some fruit ready to dip. I just have to melt the chocolate."

"Oh. My. God. Say it ain't so!" Frankie picks up the wine

and follows Rosemarie downstairs like a puppy.

They've eaten every last morsel. As evening turns to twilight, Rosemarie reminds Frankie of the purpose of their get together. Rosemarie goes to rinse her hair while Frankie sets up an impromptu salon in the dining room. Rosemarie emerges from the bathroom a few minutes later with a towel wrapped around her head. They both freeze when they hear the outside door open.

Rosemarie peeks out the window and sees her ex-boyfriend's car in the lot. When she realises that Brian has let himself in with his key, Rosemarie waits until he reaches the top of the stairs. She startles Brian by asking, "What the hell do you think you're doing?"

Brian is wearing one of those golf shirts with a corporate logo. The type of shirt Rosemarie hates, mostly because they're free. A man should buy his own clothes. His hair is messy, his eyes are glassy and he stinks of stale beer and cigars. "Rose! You scared the hell out of me. I didn't think you were home," he says.

"Obviously. Which begs the question: just what the hell *are* you doing here?"

"I just came by to pick up my sweater. I didn't see your car so I just assumed–"

"I wasn't home? You lousy sneak. Give me that key!" Rosemarie demands. Brian ignores her and heads for the bedroom. "Hand over the key and get out, Brian," she says more firmly.

"Relax, Rose, I told you I need my sweat–"

Frankie leaps across the floor. Brian hadn't noticed Frankie sitting quietly at the dining room table. Frankie is right in Brian's face, showing off a bit of assertiveness training, "No, *you* relax. The lady said get out."

"Easy, pal. You scared me for a second there. I'm Rose's boyfriend... and you are?"

"Nobody you know." Frankie says. "And just in case you're a little confused, I'm not your pal, and she's not your girlfriend."

"Well, isn't this cozy," Brian snarls, sizing up the situation.

"It's none of your concern, Brian," Rosemarie interjects. "And he's right. You're not my boyfriend, and you certainly have no right to come in here. *Especially* when you think I'm not home."

An uncomfortable silence descends over the room as the two men try to stare each other down. Each man waits for the other to make a move. Rosemarie slips away to the laundry room. "Here's your precious sweater," she says. Rosemarie drops the dripping lump of wet wool she just extracted from the washing machine into Brian's outstretched hands. Clearly, it's ruined. That's one small consolation. Rosemarie had left the washer filling when she got distracted looking for more of Brian's stuff. She had forgotten all about it until now.

Brian whines, "You washed it? It's dry clean only–"

Frankie grabs the front of Brian's shirt and shoves him roughly towards the stairs. "Take it and leave. Now!"

"Rose!" Brian pleads, "call off your dog. I'm going." He has the nerve to stop and ask, "have you got a plastic bag?"

Frankie gives Brian another little push. Brian loses his balance and clutches at the handrail to steady himself. Humiliated, Brian throws the key at Frankie's feet. Frankie does not dignify this gesture by stooping to pick it up. Brian stomps down the stairs leaving a wet trail behind him. He slams the door. The sudden rush of air does its magic trick and Frankie lets out a shriek like a little girl. Rosemarie and Frankie collapse in a fit of convulsive giggling. Choking with merriment, Frankie hollers, "And don't come back either, you son of a bitch!"

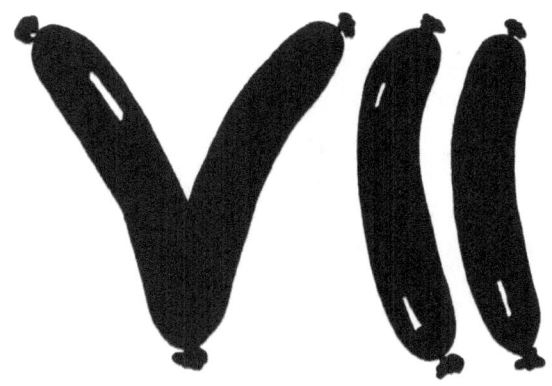

Quarter to four Sunday afternoon and Falcone's customers are shoulder to shoulder, three-deep against the display cases. The noise is deafening as Rosemarie presses through the crush to start another day at the deli. She pulls her time card out of its slot and punches in, just as John charges through the receiving doors carrying a tinfoil food pan filled with hot beef au jus. "Hey, Rose, how ya doin'? Can you give me a hand to take this order out to the customer's car?"

Rosemarie reaches for the tray John's holding but he tells her to find the order sheet to see how many buns they need. "It's for Bernard. He's waiting up at the till."

"Bernard who?

"Bernard from the McTavish," John says, "He's a regular, but I can never remember his last name."

Rosemarie's hands tremble as she searches through the orders. "I used to work for Bernard when he owned the hotel."

"Really? I didn't know that, Rosie. I'll take this up front and come back for the other tray. You grab the buns and I'll meet you there."

Holy shit! Bernard's back in town! He'll have a conniption when he sees me in this get-up. Rosemarie finds the order under "B" for Bernard: beef on a bun for twenty people—pick up 4:00 P.M. Sunday. She pulls the order, grabs three dozen buns and hurries out to face her old boss with her new boss.

Bernard waits at the front counter. As she approaches, Rosemarie sees him smirk. "Princess? Nice hat. That apron's pretty sexy, too," he says. "But what are you doing here?"

"Hi, Bernard." Rosemarie feels her colour change to match her tomato-red *Falcone* cap. "Surprised?"

"Nothing you do surprises me, Princess. You're a comedian. You can do anything."

"You mean chamaeleon."

"See. A grammar teacher, too. But I admit, I am a bit surprised to see you *here*. I heard about what happened."

"Has François been telling tales?"

"François? From the dealership? How would he know? I sat beside Tim Sandringham on the plane this morning and he told me about the shit storm you caused at the board of education."

Figures, Rosemarie thinks. Sandringham is one of the bigwigs on the board. "Oh, I thought you were talking about my car. And for the record, I didn't cause it."

"Excuse me, Bernard," John interrupts. "Rose and I will take this out to your car while you pay the cashier. Where are you parked?" John does not sound the least bit annoyed while he waits for his staff to finish chatting with a customer on one of the busiest days of the year.

"I already paid. Here, I'll take that, John. Rose can help me

96

with the rest," Bernard says, leaving no room for argument.

"Okay, Bernard. Have a great day. And thanks again for your business," John says.

As they load the hot trays into the back of Bernard's luxury SUV, he asks, "So, what about your car, Princess?"

"I couldn't afford the payments. Left it on the lot," Rosemarie explains, hoping that Bernard won't pursue this line of questioning. "François was very helpful."

"I doubt that," Bernard says. "He's a twit. The only reason I keep him around is because my daughter is in love with him. Why didn't you come to me?"

"I tried. You were out of town," Rosemarie admits. She takes advantage of this unexpected opportunity. "I heard you might be looking for someone with my skills to head up HR in your new venture."

"What new venture?" Bernard eyes Rosemarie suspiciously.

"The new marina hotel. I heard you might be involved."

"I might be. Where'd you hear that?" Bernard plays his card close to his chest. "It's supposed to be hush-hush. The City hasn't made an announcement yet."

"Sorry, Bernard, I have to get back to work. Can we get together this week and talk about it?"

"Anytime, Princess. Call me on my cell. We'll do lunch and you can tell me all your secrets," he says with yet another smirk on his face and a twinkle in his eye.

"Okay, great. I'll call you tomorrow!" Rosemarie shouts. She hurries off before Bernard's lecherous glare penetrates the back of her uniform.

The deli pulsates with throngs of people all vying for the staff's attention. Rosemarie has to elbow her way behind the meat counters. Falcone doesn't have one of those Turn-O-Matic systems, anymore. John got rid of it because the customers couldn't hear their numbers being called over the din. When a customer finally realised they'd missed their turn, it often resulted in conflict. It's not easy for the staff to determine which customer is next in line, so they rely on the honour system.

"Can I help who's next, please?" Rosemarie calls out. Three people rush forward simultaneously. "Two ribeyes!" "A stuffed-pork chop and three chicken breasts!" "A rack of back ribs!" they all order at once. And so it goes until closing-time.

The night before, Frankie had told Rosemarie that Nick hired someone who would be working the closing-shift with her tonight.

Rosemarie approaches the new girl. "Hi, I'm Rosemarie. It's been so crazy here today, I didn't get a chance to say hello yet."

"Sandy," she says, without a trace of charm. She nods at some trays of meat. "Where do these go?"

"In the walk-in cooler. We have to wrap them in plastic first, though. Follow me, and I'll show you."

While Rosemarie extricates a half-filled tray of steaks from the display case, she catches a glimpse of Timo and Nick. She sees them looking through the window that separates the customer service area and the meat cutting room, where Timo hoses down the cutting tables and floor, while Nick disassembles the equipment. They both stare back through the window at Rosemarie and Sandy.

Sandy picks up one of the trays and follows Rosemarie to the receiving area. Timo and Nick continue to watch the women work. This time they peer through the small window in the side door that leads from the meat cutting room to the receiving area. Rosemarie shows Sandy how to encase a loaded tray of steaks in plastic film using the wrapping machine, a skill she has finally mastered. As they begin to make their way through the side door past Timo and Nick and into the walk-in cooler, Rosemarie advises Sandy to be very careful on the wet floor. The combination of greasy shoes and a wet floor is always treacherous. It's even more hazardous when the staff must carry heavy trays loaded with a couple hundred dollars worth of meat. With two men watching their every move, it's unnerving. Timo kicks the cooler door open a little wider and steps aside so they can pass.

"Safety first!" Timo hollers over the racket. Besides the noise of the high-pressure sprayer and the clanking of the meat grinder parts that Nick tosses into the sink to soak, the radio is cranked up to nearly full volume.

Rosemarie and Sandy emerge from the walk-in cooler to collect the next load. Sandy volunteers to shuttle the rest of the trays if Rosemarie will wrap them.

"They're super heavy. Are you sure?" Rosemarie argues.

"Yeah, no problem. It's so fuckin' hot in here I don't mind spending some quality time inside the cooler."

Timo shucks off his smock and coils up the hose. "Hurry up, girls," he says. "Places to go, people to meet. Let's get 'er rolling, eh?" He eyes up Sandy. "Why don't you lose a layer, sister? You must be steamed."

Sandy wears a long-sleeved shirt buttoned all the way to the top and she's the only one still wearing her apron and cap. Rosemarie yanked her gear off as soon as Nick announced that the doors were locked. Both Timo and Nick are stripped down to their undershirts now.

"I'm fine, butcher boy. Don't worry about me," Sandy says.

"Easy, sister. Just tryin' to be helpful," Timo chides her.

"And I'm not your fuckin' sister," Sandy says, dressing him down in return.

Nick gives Timo a look that says *let it go*, but Timo likes a chick with some spunk and says, "Good thing, 'cause incest is one of the two things you should never try."

"Oh yeah? What's the other, butcher boy?"

"All right, you two, that's enough," Nick interjects. "Timo doesn't mean any harm, Sandy. Why don't you go help Rose wrap, then finish cleaning the display case and I'll put the rest of the meat trays away."

Nick waits until Sandy is out of ear-shot before he tells Timo, "She's having a rough time. Could you give it a rest, Mo?"

"Hey, relax Nicki. I didn't mean nothing. Just bein' friendly! That chick looks familiar though. Who is she?"

"I don't know... sister of one of Deedee's clients." Diane, or *Deedee* as Nick calls her, is Nick's girlfriend. She's a social worker and her clients are mostly young women on Mothers' Allowance who live in the nearby subsidized housing complex. "Dee says she really needs the job and doesn't mind working nights. And she's covering up some pretty impressive ink, if you must know. It's okay by me, but John says the customers find tattoos and body piercing inappropriate, so she's to keep them covered. That's why she won't strip down."

"That's it!" Timo yells. "I knew I knew that chick from somewhere! She's a peeler!"

"A what?"

"A stripper. She used to dance at Movers & Shakers. But it's *Candy*, not Sandy!"

"Oh, for crying out loud, Mo. Keep it down, will ya?" Nick implores. "She's not a stripper."

"Oh, yes, she is," Timo says reaching overhead for the stereo control. He cranks the volume up another decibel. "That's why I didn't recognized her with her clothes on. Watch this."

It doesn't take KC and The Sunshine Band more than a few bars to convince Nick that one of the women cleaning the deli is an exotic dancer.

Rosemarie is floored. She looks back and forth from Sandy to the guys staring at her colleague. Sandy shakes her booty with reckless abandon, singing along and doing things with a mop that would make a slop bucket jealous.

"Jesus, Sandy!" Rosemarie shouts over the white-boy funk, "Where'd you learn to dance like that?"

"I LOVE THIS SONG," is all Rosemarie catches before Nick turns the volume down. Timo glides through the doors singing, "That's the way, uh huh, uh huh, I like it."

They all take a fresh look at each other. "Looks clean enough to eat off," Nick says, inspecting the floor. "Let's call it a night."

"Candy's dandy, but liquor's quicker. Buy you gals a drink?" Timo oozes.

"Not me. I'm beat," Rosemarie says and doesn't stick around to find out if Timo scores.

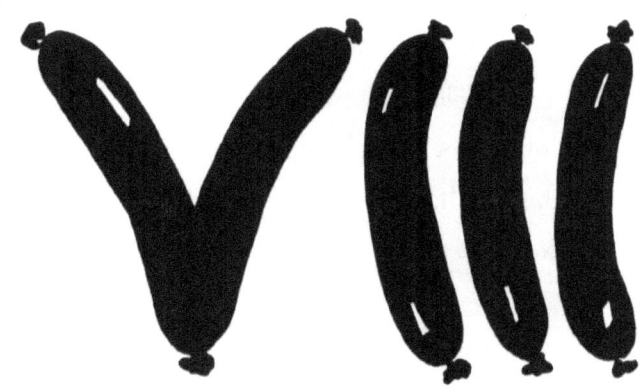

"This is Bernard speaking."

"Hi, Bernard. It's Rosemarie. Sorry, to disturb you at the office. I don't have your cell number."

"Princess! That's okay, but I can't get away for lunch until after my meeting. Can you meet me here at... what time is it now?"

"Ten to twelve."

"Oh, boy. I'm gonna be late. I gotta run. Meet me at Kelsey's at one-thirty. I should be–"

"Sorry, Bernard. No wheels. How about you pick me up and we'll grab a bite at one of the dives around here?"

"Oh, I forgot about your car. I'm super busy today. How about tomorrow? I'll pick you up. Sorry, Princess, I've got another call. I'll see you tomorrow at noon!"

And that's that. Bernard has spoken. High noon tomorrow, whether she can make it or not. When the phone rings a moment later, Rosemarie assumes that it's Bernard calling back. "Yes sir, boss man," she says.

But it's not Bernard.

"You got call display, Rose?" John asks.

"Oh, hi, John. No, sorry I thought you were someone else."

"Moonlighting, eh? Anyhow, I'm sorry to bother you on your day off, but we're in a jam and I wondered if you could help us out."

"I can't come into work today, John." Rosemarie sees a pattern developing. Although her lunch plans were just cancelled, she doesn't want John to make this a habit. "I have to get a lot of things done today," she says. "Especially since I'm not sure what my schedule is for the rest of the week."

"I understand, Rose, and I did the schedule last night–you're not scheduled in until Wednesday. Unless you want to work tomorrow, you've got two days off in a row. I'm calling to ask if you can come in to give me a hand with the payroll," John explains. "Lina's still off, but we have to pay the staff. It shouldn't take long, Rose. And I know you could do it a lot faster than me."

"Oh, I see. I guess your mom's not feeling better yet?" Rosemarie ventures. John doesn't respond and there's a long pause until she finally agrees. Rosemarie needs to get paid today like everybody else.

"You're a lifesaver, Rose. Thanks a million." Before Rosemarie can ask John how much a lifesaver makes, he hangs up.

Rosemarie finds John in his office. He looks tired. Rosemarie asks John about his mom again and finds out that Frankie's worries are justified. No wonder John looks so tired. John admits that he's very worried about his mother. He tells Rosemarie that Lina has been admitted into St. Joseph's for monitoring and he's been trying to cover for her while doing everything else he normally does, which is a lot!

"I was thinking, Rose. If you could take over some of Lina's duties I could double your wage while you're working in the office," John says.

Although it still won't come close to what Rosemarie was making at the board, she jumps at the offer. "I'd love to John, at least until I find something more suitable," she says. Rosemarie finds clerical work so much easier than physical labour, and a lot less stressful than trying to please fickle customers.

"Okay, great. We'll start when you come to work on Wednesday, if that's okay with you," John says.

Rosemarie doesn't want to waste John's time, or her own. She asks John for the time cards so she can start on the payroll. John asks Rosemarie to call him when she's finished. He relinquishes his seat and tells Rosemarie again how much he appreciates her coming in on short notice.

Rosemarie doesn't mind doing the payroll. In fact it's more in her line of work. And now that her feet aren't killing her (thanks to Sam's growth spurt), she's beginning to enjoy working in the meat department, too. At least there's always lots of interesting people coming and going. Even if they're cantankerous, it makes the time pass quickly. At the board, Rosemarie spent long hours sitting alone at her desk working on tasks that would be considered very boring by some of her new co-workers' standards.

Rosemarie has little difficulty calculating the deductions manually. Only a handful of the employees are full-time. The majority are part-time workers and there's a lot more of them than she thought. Nonetheless, she finishes the job efficiently in a little more than two hours. She discovers that John doesn't take home any more money than his cousins, although he works a lot harder and carries most of the responsibility. None of them are paid as well as most of the teachers Rosemarie hired straight out of university. And the Falcones sure don't get the summer off. In fact they work harder because everyone else takes vacation.

Using the phone on Lina's desk, Rosemarie calls John on the intercom. He says he'll be with her in a minute. While she waits, Rosemarie takes a second look through the stack of cheques she just issued and notices that she didn't make one for Sandy. Rosemarie flips through the time cards and can't find Sandy's.

"Hey, Rose, that was fast. Any problems?" John leans over the desk and signs the first cheque in the stack.

"Just that I don't have a timecard for Sandy so I didn't make a cheque for her."

"That's cause we don't have a timecard for her. She didn't fill in her paperwork yet and now Nick says she isn't coming back."

"What do you mean, she isn't coming back? I worked with her last night, she seemed to be doing okay."

"Yeah, I know. I thought so too, but Nick called this morning in a panic. He says Sandy's sister told Deedee she's gone and that it's all Timo's fault."

"Timo?" Rosemarie doesn't know what to think of that. She saw the way Timo was looking at Sandy. *Lasciviously*, she thinks. She wonders now what Timo might have done to scare a tough woman like Sandy away. "What did he do?" she asks.

"I have no idea," John admits. "But I intend to find out just as soon as I can get a hold of him."

"Well, you can at least pay her for the hours she worked," Rosemarie says. "I know she worked till eleven last night, and Nick should be able to tell you her hours for Saturday."

"But we don't even know her last name, let alone social insurance number. She didn't fill in the paperwork," John reiterates. He sounds a bit annoyed.

"Well, does Nick know where Sandy lives?"

"Yeah. He said she's staying with her sister. Her sister is a regular customer. They live over in that building for unwed mothers."

Unwed mothers? Where does he get this stuff? "You mean the City's subsidized housing complex for single mothers? The one just down the street?"

"Yeah. That's the one," John confirms.

"You can pay cash for casual labour if she's not coming back," Rosemarie tells John. "As long as it's less than $700." Rosemarie knows the labour laws and she assumes that Sandy must need the money or she wouldn't have taken a job like this. Nobody works that hard for fun.

"Wow, Rose, you're really something. I didn't think of that. Do you think you could take the cash to her since you know where she lives? I'd really appreciate it."

"I guess so, John," she agrees. "So long as you trust me."

"Course I do, Rosie. I'll call Nick and find out how many hours she worked on Saturday."

Although Rosemarie walks past this housing complex on her way home from work, she's never stepped foot inside the gate before. The City of Thunder Bay own a number of inconspicuous residences in the neighbourhood. This one is designated for single mothers and their children, so it's always full of little kids playing outside. Rosemarie looks around and notices all the women staring at her. She has seen some of them shopping at Falcone during the evenings when the clientele changes to a more motley collection of people who come in to buy cold cut ends and pieces, reduced to sell before John donates them to the soup kitchen. Before Rosemarie can ask anyone for directions, one of the women–who looks a lot like Sandy–heads straight for her with a kid in tow.

Must be the sister, Rosemarie guesses. "Hi, I'm–"

"I know who you are," the young woman says with unmistakable hostility. "Whaddaya want?"

Rosemarie remembers her from the deli. The skinny one with the flaming red hair who always orders sun-dried tomato-basil turkey breast. "I'm looking for Sandy."

"Yeah? You and everybody else!" she snarls, yanking the toddler right off her feet. "Alla you Falcone people can go to hell. And you better hope somebody else doesn't find her first, or I'll hold it against you personally!"

Rosemarie is baffled. "Me? Why would you hold it against me? I just want to deliver her pay," Rosemarie tries to explain. "She didn't leave any info, not even an address, but I heard her sister lives here. I thought I might be able to help. We worked together last night."

"Give it to me," the sister demands. She holds out one mitt and has the other one clamped around the kid who starts to whine.

"Ow, Mommy! That hurts," her kid cries.

"Oh, sorry, baby. Go play. Mommy needs to talk."

"Cute kid," Rosemarie says, sarcasm being one of her favourite toys. "What's her name?"

"What's it to you? Give me the pay cheque," she demands again.

"No can do." Rosemarie refuses. She's not about to give the cash to a stranger. "If you see Sandy, tell her I have some cash for her. Here's my number." Rosemarie tears the stub off her own cheque and scribbles her phone number.

"Cash?"

"I told you, she didn't leave any information, so I talked the boss into paying her cash for the two days she worked."

"Really? Is that true?" Her eyes are aglow and she sounds more amicable now that she's heard that magic word.

"Yup, casual labour. He can pay her cash."

"Well, that's a horse's ass of a different colour. Amber!" she shouts at her kid. "Go get Aunty Sandy. Tell her a nice lady wants to see her!"

"Pipe down, idiot. I'm right here." Sandy materialises from somewhere behind the swing set. "What's up, Rose? I'm kinda layin' low."

"Hi Sandy. Nick says you're not coming back and I just wanted you to get paid. I'm on my way home." Rosemarie hopes that Sandy won't be as hostile as her sister. "I just live down the street."

"That's right neighbourly of ya," Sandy says, mocking Rosemarie. "My sister here is just trying to keep trouble away. And wherever I am, there's bound to be trouble. You know what I mean?"

Rosemarie does not know what she means. "Timo do something to you?" she asks. She doesn't want to believe that part is true.

"That fuckin' butcher? He recognized me, is all. Can't have that. Now, what was that about cash?" Sandy asks.

Rosemarie can't help but notice that Sandy looks a lot different without the *Falcone* gear. Most women do, but not because of its inability to flatter. This woman is covered, absolutely covered, in tattoos! Rosemarie has never seen anything like it. "He recognized you?"

"Hard to believe, eh? Amy Winehouse could hide out in that *Falcone* get up if she didn't want to get found. Guess I shouldn't have put on such a good show last night. Can't help myself when the tunes rock, ya know?"

"What are you, on the lam or something?" Rosemarie jokes, regretting the words the moment they are spoken.

"Yeah, but you're not the one I'm worried about. That butcher opens his mouth, there's gonna be a lot of trouble. I seen him when I was dancing at Movers & Shakers. He could yap to the people I *am* worried about, and before you know it, I got all of Satan's little helpers over here. Meanwhile, much as I'd like to invite you in for tea, it'd be better if you handed over the dough and get yourself gone. You know what I mean?"

Rosemarie still doesn't know what she means. Probably never will. "Okay, here's your money." She hands Sandy an envelope. "You should have earned another 4% for vacation pay, but at least there's no deductions."

Sandy grabs the envelope and eyeballs her benefactor while

she counts the cash. "Sweet." With that, the tattooed work of art vanishes.

Rosemarie is half-way down the street when Sandy's sister catches up with her. "That was weird," she says. "I mean it was *nice*, but it was weird. Can I ask you a question? About the cash, I mean."

"Yeah, what about it?" Rosemarie's a little leery herself now.

"Well, you seem to know all the tricks and I was wondering if it would work for me, too."

"Well, um... what's your name?"

"Oh," she says, and sticks out her hand. "I'm Autumn Dawn, but my friends just call me Dawn."

"Rosemarie. My friends call me everything but."

"What a strange name." Dawn frowns and looks confused.

"Well, Dawn... can I call you Dawn? It's not a trick."

"Sure. Autumn Dawn's my stage name. Can I call you Rosemarie?"

Wow, this could take a while. "What is it you want to ask me about?"

"How I can get paid cash. Deedee, that's my social worker, she said that I have to find a job, and I can't go back to being a dancer, now that I've got a kid I can't work nights and sleep all day, but if I get a job, I gotta pay back half, so there's no point really, but I was thinking, if Candy got paid cash, then maybe I can, too."

"Who's Candy?" Talking to Dawn is more confusing than talking to her sister.

"Sandy. Candy's her stage name."

Rosemarie is starting to get the picture. "So if you could get paid like Candy–I mean Sandy–you could continue to collect benefits," Rosemarie says, pleased with herself for deciphering what Deedee told Dawn.

"I don't get any benefits. I'm on Mothers' Allowance," Dawn clarifies. "And I'm supposed to be looking for a job but it's kinda hard with no experience, or at least not the type you can put on your resumation," she explains.

"Well, Dawn. Like I said, it's not a trick. The reason Ca–Sandy got paid cash, is because she won't be coming back to work. It's a one-off. If you got a job at Falcone, they'd have to make deductions and report your earnings to Canada Revenue."

"Wow, you're ever smart," Dawn says. Clearly, she's impressed by Rosemarie's simple explanation. "But I can't do that. I still wouldn't make enough to support my kid, and they'd cut me off the dole, which is bad enough, but I'd have to find somewhere else to live, too."

"Sorry, Dawn. Wish I could help, but I gotta get going." Rosemarie has her own problems, yet can't imagine having it as bad as these women seem to have it.

"'Kay. Nice talking to you, Everything But, I mean, *Rosemarie*. Oh, and don't say nothing to Deedee 'cause I told her Sandy's gone. Another stupid rule! She's not supposed to be living here. Besides, she'll be gone as soon as the bikers get wind of it, now that that stupid butcher knows."

A thought crosses Rosemarie's mind. Something about glass houses and stones, but she keeps quiet and keeps walking. She's eager to end this confusing encounter without finding out what bikers could possibly have to do with it. It hits her before she makes it home. Bikers control the strip clubs. And it's tough travelling incognita wearing nothing but radically distinctive graphic art.

Once Rosemarie finally frees herself from the stripper-sisters, she rushes to the bank to deposit her own pay cheque.

She spends the rest of the afternoon sorting out her finances. With the increase in pay from doing Lina's job she just might be able to make the rent. The problem is that it's due before next payday. Stalling the landlord for even a day or two isn't an option because he has Rosemarie's post-dated cheques and he's out of the country. She dreads meeting with him next month when her lease expires. Rosemarie is afraid her landlord won't renew her lease once he finds out she lost her high-paying job.

Rosemarie can't think of any other way to make up the shortfall so she decides she'll have to accept her sister's offer. She calls Roseanna and tells her that she needs a short-term loan and will be able to pay her back in installments every payday. Roseanna says she doesn't care if it takes forever, but Rosemarie is determined to support herself without getting any further into debt.

Unless she moves out, Rosemarie will have to find a roommate. She's also worried about what the landlord will have to say about that. When her landlord saw Brian's car in the lot early one morning, he stopped Rosemarie on her way to work and made it clear that he wouldn't tolerate additional tenants without his consent. Instead of telling him that it was one of the rare occasions when her boyfriend stayed overnight, she told him Brian was out of town and she was using his car. She waited until the landlord left before she got into her own car. Rosemarie didn't like being dishonest with him, but she also didn't think it was any of his business. She assumes he'd raise the rent if Brian, or anyone else were to move in.

Rosemarie only stops in at Falcone to grab a bite because she was supposed to go for lunch with Bernard but he cancelled, again. Angie, who is just back from holidays and unaware that Rosemarie is staff, makes her a sandwich. Rosemarie gets the distinct impression that Angie isn't pleased about being back at work, so Rosemarie doesn't bother to introduce herself. She opts to wait until they work together.

"They should have eighty-sixed that," the cashier tells Rosemarie.

"Why? There's nothing wrong with the porchetta, they just opened it this morning."

"No, I mean they should have used code 86. Staff get sandwiches at cost when they're off duty. I'll have to charge you the regular price now, unless you want to go back and get them to weigh it again. I can't change the code from here, only Lina can. All I can do is give you your staff discount," the cashier says sympathetically.

Rosemarie rarely has the opportunity to chat with the cashiers and doesn't know this one's name yet. As Rosemarie discovered when she issued their pay cheques the day before, the cashiers don't make a lot either.

"That's okay, I'm kind of in a hurry. I will next time, though, thanks."

Rosemarie leaves feeling optimistic. If she can land that HR position with Bernard, she won't have to worry about the price of porchetta. Meanwhile, she's going to earn a little more money when she takes over some of Lina's duties.

Later that day, with plenty of things she'd rather be doing put on hold, Rosemarie plans to look at the one-bedroom apartment she saw advertised on the staff bulletin board. It's located in the neighbourhood close to the store and it's available immediately for a little more than half what she's paying now. She calls the number and is a bit surprised to find out it's one of Timo's properties. Rosemarie makes an appointment to view the place and agrees to meet Timo at the store after work.

She arrives just as John pulls into the parking lot. He's returning to work after a short break to take over for Timo. During their conversation over dinner, Frankie told Rosemarie that John likes to have a meat cutter on in the evenings, although Timo is the only certified butcher on staff. When they graduated from high school, John started working full-time in the family business while Timo apprenticed at A&P. According to Frankie, John thought it would bring more customers into the store if they sold fresh meat, but his father disagreed. He told John that all butchers are alcoholics or perverts, sometimes both, and he wouldn't have one working for him. After Giuseppe died and John took over management, he offered Timo a job. Timo didn't hesitate, said he hated working at

A&P. He was sick of working with a bunch of alcoholics and perverts. Timo taught John and Nick what they need to know about butchering, and since they don't normally do much meat cutting after six o'clock, Nick can cover any special requests in the evening.

This is Nick's night off, so John is working a split shift. Frankie is still hanging around. He seems eager to talk to Rosemarie and pounces on her as soon as she walks in.

"Hey, doll face, why didn't you tell me you were thinking of moving out?"

"Hi, Rose," Timo says. "Frankie's been yapping about what a great place you got over there. Hope you don't think this joint I've got for rent is gonna be anything like that."

"Hi, guys. I'm not a hundred percent sure of anything yet, especially moving, but my lease expires next month." Responding to Timo, Rosemarie says, "I know I'll never find another place like the apartment I'm in now. I just want to take a look around in case my landlord won't renew my lease."

"Nothin' he can do about it," Timo says.

Rosemarie finds that hard to believe. "Besides, I can't afford the rent anymore unless I find a roommate, but he might not allow it. Either that, or he'll raise the rent," she explains.

"Can't do that, neither," Timo states with the confidence and authority of someone who knows what he's talking about. For many years Timo has made a decent living as a landlord. He owns multiple dwellings scattered throughout the city.

"You don't know my landlord, Timo. He's kind of a hard case."

"Don't matter, it's what the RTA says that counts."

"What's the RTA?" Frankie and Rosemarie ask in stereo.

"Residential Tenancy Act." Timo is well-versed in the rules governing landlords and tenants in Ontario. "Check it out for yourself. Here," he says, handing Rosemarie an information bulletin. "I'm obliged to provide prospective tenants with one of these. Your landlord should've given you one when you signed a lease. He can't make you move out when it expires, he has no say about who you live with, and he sure as shit can't raise the rent because of it."

"Wow, Timo. I had no idea!"

"Yeah, most tenants don't. They changed the law in Ontario a few years ago to protect people from unscrupulous landlords. Now there's fuck-all a landlord can do to get rid of lousy tenants unless he can prove they're carrying on illegal activities or severely overcrowding the unit. You get some of these foreigners bringing over every relative they got, and pretty soon you got about a dozen people living in a place built for two. And you can't ask 'em anything personal, like, 'have you got seventeen cousins livin' in there?' They go crying to the Ontario Human Rights Commission and nail your balls to the wall. Accuse you of racism. Believe me, I seen it all. I had a deadbeat junkie that never paid the rent till I got a writ and the sheriff came to evict her. Then she just pays the rent and we do the whole routine again next month. Went on for a couple years like that till she finally OD'ed."

"You're kidding!" Frankie marvels. "Couldn't you just cut off the hydro or something?"

"No way. I can't even take a security deposit. I'm telling you, it's not easy being a slumlord! The RTA is written totally in favour of the tenant. That's why I'm so picky about who I rent to."

"So, you're telling me that I don't have to renew my lease and I can get a roommate if I want to?"

"That's what I'm telling you, Rose. You still wanna look at my unit?"

"Wait!" Frankie interrupts. He lunges at Rosemarie. "Can I talk to you for a sec?"

"Make it quick, Frankie," says Timo, "I got stuff to do and can't hang around here while you two have a heart to heart. I'll be outside when you're ready, Rose."

Frankie talks so fast, Rosemarie can scarcely understand what he's saying. Something about him moving in. She can practically see a lightbulb hovering over Frankie's head. "You mean you'll take over my place if I take Timo's?"

"No. I mean I'll be your roommate," Frankie volunteers. "I'm very tidy and that place is definitely big enough. And I've been thinking of moving out since Nick starting making noise about getting married."

"Slow down, Frankie. Let me think about it. I'm still in shock over what Timo said and now you tell me Nick's getting married?"

"Of course, no problem. I just don't want you to lose that place, doll. And I'd love to live there, too. Who wouldn't? And Nick's only been thinking about marriage—he hasn't asked Deedee yet, so please don't say anything."

"Okay, Frankie. I'll think it over. I'll go tell Timo to forget about it for now. I've wasted enough of his time already."

Frankie leaves Rosemarie to ponder his offer, skipping gleefully out the back door like he just caught the bouquet at his brother's wedding.

Rosemarie apologizes to Timo for keeping him waiting and thanks him for the information. She leaves before Timo can bill her for consulting services.

Maybe it would be okay if Frankie moved in with her. Rosemarie is very fond of Frankie and now that she doesn't have to worry about what the landlord has to say, she seriously considers it. It would solve her immediate problems; she wouldn't have to move out and it would cut her rent in half. Will it bring new challenges? Rosemarie can't think of any reason not to let Frankie move in. So what if he's a guy, Rosemarie would prefer living with Frankie over any number of women she knows, none of whom would be interested in living on Superior Street. Besides that, Rosemarie suspects Frankie is gay. In fact, she can't think of a better scenario. He's easy to get along with, he's gainfully employed and he likes to cook. It doesn't take Rosemarie long to decide it's a good offer. When she gets home, Rosemarie calls the store and asks John for Frankie's number.

The next morning, Rosemarie feels like she's on top of the world, or at least on top of her own problems. She hurries to work. John introduces Rosemarie to Angie, who doesn't look nearly as eager as Rosemarie is. Angie didn't say much, except that her vacation was too short when Carol asked her about it. Rosemarie got the impression Angie resents having to return to work at all. As soon as they start to prep for lunch, John whisks Rosemarie downstairs to get started on the books, leaving her glum colleagues to handle the more tedious chores.

Rosemarie listens attentively as John explains his mother's accounting system. Rosemarie avoids personal matters and limits her queries to the tasks at hand. And she has plenty of questions to pose on that topic. What a mess! By mid-morning, Rosemarie is almost able to decipher Lina's method, which only vaguely follows the standard principles of accounting she was taught in her business class at Lakehead University.

Rosemarie leaves the crazy books in a mild state of confusion to go help with the lunch rush. She forgot to put her *Falcone* cap on, until Mervin notices.

"Hey, nice haircut, Miss."

"Thanks, Mervin. Frankie did it."

All eyes are on Rosemarie while she tucks her hair up under her cap and grabs a pair of disposable gloves. John smiles from the meat cutting room where he works with Timo cutting steaks. Normally the cutting room is separated from the customer service area by a glass window which can be lifted, as it is now. This enables them to pass orders through and reach the telephone from either side. John and Timo exchange a few words that Rosemarie can't quite make out. She senses that they are talking about her.

Rosemarie notices a new slicer where the old one had been. Mervin tells Rosemarie that John replaced it because he was worried about the staff not using the pusher block on the old one. "The old one was better," Mervin complains, "it did a better job on cheese." According to Mervin, the slicer was obsolete and John couldn't get parts. The new one has a lightweight lexan pusher block. As soon as she tries it, Rosemarie realizes that they don't make them like they used to. That old workhorse had a bigger motor and could stand up to the resistance that cheese puts on the blade.

John asks Rosemarie how she likes the new slicer. "I just sharpened the blade, Rose. How's it cutting?"

"It's great, John. What happened to the old one?"

"I sent it down to the prep room for doing meat and cheese trays," John says. Rosemarie gives him a thumbs up and forces herself to look away. She's shamed by her previous opinion on matters she knew so little about.

Carol gives Rosemarie a dark, accusatory look. Rosemarie adjusts her cap and blushes. She remembers their heated conversation about replacing the slicer following Tracey's accident.

A customer approaches the counter. Before Rosemarie can greet him, the man demands to see the sausage maker. Frankie steps forward. "Many of us make the sausage here, sir. How can I help you?"

"I got a complaint. Your sausage is full of filler and the label here doesn't say what's in it." The angry customer throws a package of sausage that's been ripped open onto the counter. He folds his arms across his massive chest like a trial lawyer at his closing argument.

"Well, sir, our labels list exactly what is contained in all our products. Only our breakfast sausage contains filler. I can assure you we don't use any filler in our Italian sausage. It contains one hundred percent pork and seasoning, just like it says here on the label," Frankie explains.

John watches this exchange while Timo sharpens his fourteen inch butcher knife with more exuberance than the task strictly calls for. Steel scraping against steel, an eerie sound intended to intimidate.

"That's bullshit," the customer says loudly. He looks eager for confrontation. "Lemme see the boss."

John gives Timo a slight nod and that's all it takes to send the mad butcher charging through the double doors. Wielding his sharpened weapon, Timo is ready for battle. "You got a problem here, Frankie?" Timo asks, while his steely blue eyes pierce the customer.

"No, not really. I was just explaining to this um... gentleman, that our Italian sausage does not contain filler and he, um... thinks otherwise."

"Yeah, I got a problem," the customer chimes in. "This clown can say whatever he wants, but I know there's filler in 'em."

All eyes are on Timo now. Silence fills the room while he waits a beat or two. Timo allows the tension to build until he has the surly customer's undivided attention. Without breaking eye contact, Timo leans forward until he's right in the guy's face and says "First of all, he's not a clown, and I'd appreciate it if you would show a little respect. And secondly, like the man said, there's no filler in our sausage. If you don't believe him *that's* your problem."

He's no match for Timo's towering bulk, yet the recalcitrant consumer is not put off by this show of strength and solidarity. He stands up a little taller and shouts, "Oh, yeah? I think it's *you* that's got a problem." In a failed attempt to rally support from the growing audience, he warns, "You can't go around printing lies on your label."

Timo slams his knife down on the counter for effect and says, "Look, this conversation is not doing *you* any good, and it's certainly not doing *me* any good so it's over."

Timo continues to stare him down until his opponent backs off. Defeated, the customer mumbles a few curses as he shambles out of the store. When the door shuts behind him, Timo picks up his knife, winks at Rosemarie and struts back to work. A collective sigh relieves the pressure and everyone returns to their various tasks.

"What the hell was that all about?" Rosemarie asks Mervin.

"Who knows. Timo the Conqueror showing off a little, maybe. That guy comes in here all the time and always gives us a hard time. He's never happy.

"That guy gave me a hard time, too. He didn't like the steaks I sold him and claimed that, 'Old Man Falcone would be spinning in his grave if he saw them.' I thought I had done something wrong," Rosemarie says.

"Well, he was right about *that*, Rose," Frankie interjects. "Uncle Giuseppe would have been vexed, but not for that reason."

"Frankie's right," Carol says. When Giuseppe was alive we didn't sell fresh meat. He wouldn't let us."

"Wouldn't let us, what?" John asks. "What are you guys talking about."

"The Sexist," Mervin says, looking proud because he remembered Timo's nickname for that pushy customer.

Timo joins in. "It's *Sexpert*, Merv," Timo says, shaking his head. "As in 'sexual expert.' Guy's a fucking know it all."

"All right, Mo. We still got a lot of customers to look after. Can I help somebody over here?" John asks.

***

124

Rosemarie returns to the office to take another stab at the pile of paperwork. It's a relief to be out of the crush of customer service. By mid-afternoon, Rosemarie has organized the accounts payable by due date, calculated the payroll source deductions and completed the forms for reporting to Canada Revenue. In an attempt to figure out how Lina does the bank deposits, Rosemarie looks over some of the previous deposit slips. She finds cash register tapes corresponding to the sum of the deposit slip they're attached to. Rosemarie adds up the current stack of sales receipts and completes the CIBC deposit slip, filling in the corresponding sums of cash, cheques, credit card and debit card transactions. When she's finished, Rosemarie tucks it all into the safe and closes it securely. Done! Rosemarie shuts off the lights and goes upstairs to find John. She wants to ask him if he can take a look at the deposit before he goes to the bank.

Rosemarie asks Gord if he's seen John. Gord tells her that John went to see his mom and left instructions for him to drive Rosemarie to the bank with the deposit, then take her home. "Oh, oh," Gord says when Rosemarie tells him that she locked the deposit in the safe. "Better leave him a note." Gord offers to give Rosemarie a ride home anyhow. Gord is ready to go, and he's accustomed to driving Lina to the bank before taking her home at the end of every day. When Rosemarie hesitates, Gord assures her it's no problem. "Boss's orders," he says.

During the short ride home, Rosemarie asks Gord if they've always used the same bank. She has to shout to be heard. The radio's speakers are blaring Pink Floyd's moral indignation toward greed. *Money so they say, is the root of all evil today. But if you ask for a rise it's no surprise that they're giving none away.* It's not surprising to learn that there's only one bank for Lina Falcone. Every Italian-Canadian Rosemarie has ever known does their banking at the CIBC, mattresses notwithstanding. When Rosemarie opened her first bank account she found out the "I" in CIBC stood for *Imperial.* Until then, Rosemarie had assumed it was the Canadian-Italian Bank of Commerce.

"You kidding, Rose?" Gord replies between verses. "Lina's a creature of habit." So is Gord, Rosemarie speculates.

Rosemarie forgot all about paying for her mom's peppers. John must have, too. He doesn't seem to be himself lately. Rosemarie supposes it must be because of all the stress. With his mother off, John has been working around the clock, and as Gord told Rosemarie, Lina usually handles the seasonal sales of bulk stuff. Rosemarie noticed a lot of spoiled peppers tossed out on the loading dock when she came in to work. Several more pressing matters need to be addressed, too.

Running a small business has a lot of challenges. With so many important tasks performed by so few, when even one person is missing, like Lina, or distracted, like John, their absence can be devastating. Rosemarie vows to be as helpful as she can while she's at work and looks forward to the day she's back within the less hectic hierarchy she was accustomed to at the school board.

Rosemarie hopes to make some progress before the next lunch rush. She settles herself behind the desk and spots the note she scribbled in haste yesterday, right where she left it. Before she can begin to sort through the mound of paperwork that's accumulated in Lina's absence, John plops down into the other chair.

"Morning, Rose." John picks up the post-it note stuck to the phone and glances up at the safe. "I guess I should go to the bank before I forget," John says.

"Sorry, John. I didn't know you wanted me to make the bank deposit. I locked up."

"That's okay, I should have asked you first. I should be thanking you for having the smarts to do that."

"Security's tight," Rosemarie jokes. "I know you're busy, John, but I do need a little more guidance. Can we have a quick chat when you get back?"

"Sure. Now's good. What's up?"

"Well, for starters I didn't pay for the peppers I took."

"Oh, yeah. I forgot about that. Which reminds me," John reaches into his back pocket and retrieves a bulging envelope. "Here's some money from pepper sales," John tells his temporary bookkeeper. He throws it on top of the pile. "The invoice and freight bill are in there, too."

"How much were they, John? I'll add the money for my mom's case to the deposit."

"That's okay, Rose. Never mind, you earned them. Besides, I had to throw a lot away. For some unknown reason a lot of people cancelled their orders and the peppers spoiled."

"Yeah, I noticed that. What a shame. Anyhow, I'm sure my mom will appreciate that. Thanks. I also wondered if you want me to do ROE's for Randy and Tiffany. I'm pretty sure there's probably a deadline... I don't suppose Lina–"

"Nope. I forgot about that, too. I'm nearly as forgetful as she is," John admits, "and that's pretty bad."

"How is she?"

"Not good. It doesn't look like she'll be coming back to work anytime soon."

"Oh, I'm sorry, John. I know how hard this has been on you. Finding someone to take over for Lina won't be easy."

"Yeah, we'll figure something out. Don't worry, Rose. Meanwhile, if you could keep things rolling, I might be able to muddle through it."

"Well, that's another thing I want to talk to you about, John. I'm happy to help out until you can find someone else to do it, full-time, I mean. And by the way, I'm not sure how you want me to keep track of my time."

"Me neither, Rose."

"I was only up front for the lunch rush yesterday and I see there's still a lot to be done here." Rosemarie doesn't sugar-coat it. "And you're probably going to have trouble finding a bookkeeper that can make sense of it."

"Is it that bad?"

Seeing the look on John's face change from optimistic to distressed, Rosemarie decides against adding to his worries, at least for now. "Why don't you go to the bank and we'll talk about it later. Oh, before you go, John, can you take a look at the deposit to make sure I've done it correctly?"

"Did it balance with the cash register tapes?"

"It did. How do I enter the sales for the peppers?"

"I'm not sure, maybe you can look back at how Lina handled the tomatoes last month," John suggests.

"Okay, I'll do that. Thanks."

"And I'll let you know how many we had to eighty-six when I talk to Gord," John says.

"What do you want me to do about that?"

"I think you make a journal entry to deduct it from our cost of goods," John says. "Just like anything with code 86. At least that's how Lina does it, I think."

It certainly is an appropriate code number, Rosemarie muses. She doesn't claim to have an eidetic memory, and Rosemarie's own system of mnemonic triggers, clever as it might have initially seemed, lacked consistency. The only way she's been able to commit most of the accursed code to memory is by good old-fashioned repetition. "Isn't that the code we use for staff sandwiches?"

"Yeah, and anything spoiled," John confirms.

"That doesn't make sense, John."

"Hardly anything makes sense to me lately," John confesses. "And to be honest, accounting is one of those mysteries I never really understood."

Once John leaves, Rosemarie counts the money he said was for peppers. She searches through the cash receipts and doesn't find any transactions for peppers or anything entered with code 86, yet the bank deposit balances with the cash register tapes. Rosemarie scours the previous month's deposit slips and examines Lina's corresponding entries in last month's general ledger. She finds a single entry to credit "cost of goods" and debit "spoilage." Still confused, Rosemarie adds up all the sales of products entered with code 86 for that month, a time-consuming task that she finds tedious. She discovers that the sum corresponds with Lina's journal entry. Rosemarie searches again; she peruses the previous month's sales receipts looking for bulk sales of tomatoes. Nada. Frustrated, Rosemarie remembers posting the supplier's invoice and locates it to check the date. When she looks at the cash register tapes for the days immediately following the arrival of tomatoes, Rosemarie finds several entries made with a code number that she's not familiar with. The sales are mostly for thirty dollars, a few for sixty, sometimes ninety. Rosemarie assumes these must be the bulk sales of tomatoes. She uses the bulk code to enter the sales of peppers and adds the cash to the deposit.

Rosemarie can't believe how antiquated Falcone's accounting system is. They could save so much time if they were to implement a simple computerized bookkeeping program. Even if it's not integrated with inventory control, it would improve efficiency ten-fold. Considering how everything else in the store has been modernized, the more Rosemarie thinks about it, the more she can't understand why they haven't updated, unless....

Rosemarie has a sudden realisation. Somebody came into the office yesterday looking for Lina. He was acting very odd and wouldn't say what it was he wanted, although he made it clear that he would only deal with Lina. When Rosemarie told him Lina wouldn't be back for a while, the man left in a huff. Now she recalls seeing that same old guy wandering around the store last Sunday afternoon asking for Lina. Rosemarie was too busy to get involved and directed him to John. Then she saw the man slip out through the back. Rosemarie now suspects that he wanted to pay cash, under the table, no tax, no receipt. Who knows? She could be wrong.

Rosemarie also suspects that Lina's accounting system covers a multitude of "errors" which would explain Lina's disdain for computers. It's a common fallacy that computers eliminate paperwork when in fact they create a paper trail that can be easily followed by an amateur, like John. Or an expert, like an auditor. Rosemarie decides she better take a closer look at the books and maybe find some forensic proof before she accuses John's mother of larceny.

Moving day and Rosemarie is almost as excited as Frankie is. She offers to help Frankie pack boxes but he tells her he's got everything ready to go. Frankie has lived in the same house since he and Nick were kids. He doesn't seem sad to be leaving Nick, in fact, Frankie appears to be in a hurry.

Rosemarie's apartment is fully furnished so Frankie didn't need to bring anything but his personal belongings. It doesn't take long to carry Frankie's stuff up from his car. Rosemarie makes a pot of tea and the two of them sit down to relax and talk. Rosemarie asks Frankie to tell her a little more about his family. She knows John's dad died sometime after high school, but she doesn't know anything about what happened to Frankie and Nick's parents.

Although Frankie seems reluctant at first, once he starts to talk about it, a lot of half-forgotten memories surface. Rosemarie can tell that Frankie really misses Lina. Frankie tells Rosemarie that Lina raised them from the time he and Nick were babies because their mother died. Rosemarie waits for more about his mother's death, but Frankie doesn't elaborate. Then Frankie tells Rosemarie that when he and Nick were still only little kids their father died unexpectedly of a massive heart attack. Their cousin, John was just a baby. While the rest of the family was in a terrible state of shock and confusion, Lina demonstrated an uncommon amount of strength and compassion.

"Lina always treated me and Nick like we were her own kids. She was a great mother to us in spite of having to work full-time and care for Uncle Giuseppe. He was a heavy smoker and sick for many years." It's hard for Rosemarie to believe that Frankie is describing the same man that had been an aerial performer with the circus—a catcher, John had told her.

"After our dad died, Uncle Giuseppe lost all interest in life and stopped looking after himself," Frankie explains. "And the less he did, the more Aunt Lina had to. It was very difficult for her," Frankie says with such sadness that Rosemarie can almost see the grief wrapped around him like a well-worn blanket.

Just when Rosemarie thinks the conversation has ended, Frankie surprises her by continuing. "Tessa—that's our mother—had some sort of hold over them all. When she died, it changed all their lives. None of them were the same people they were back in the old country. Lina used to tell us stories about the circus when we were sick or needed cheering up. She'd wake us up late at night to watch reruns of *Trapeze* when it came on TV. 'Come and see your mother dressed up like Gina Lollobrigida,' she'd say. Of course we thought Lina made that up until she showed us one of the costumes she had made for Tessa. Lina kept all the costumes in an old steamer trunk up in her sewing room in the attic. None of us were allowed in there and it was always locked. Sometimes Lina would disappear for hours on end and we knew she wasn't sewing, but we had no idea what she was up to. Then one night Lina hauled the whole lot down from the attic and showed us this one costume. It was exactly, I mean in every detail, exactly the same as the one the famous movie star was wearing in the film."

Frankie's eyes light up as he continues his tale. "As I said, Lina kept the attic locked and kept all her keys on a key-ring that she hung on her bedside lamp when she came home from work. I remember one day Nick and I were home from school. I felt fine, but Nick had the mumps or something so she kept us both home... twins, you know. Anyhow, I was bored and while Aunt Lina was busy I snuck into her room and took the keys. She caught me playing around with the costumes and I'd never seen her so angry. She threatened to beat me if I ever touched that trunk again."

"Wow, Frankie, that is so sad and so strange. I had no idea. Do you think Lina has been suffering from depression?"

"I think it's more than depression. Either way, she needs a rest. She's been working too hard for too long."

"I just hope John can find someone to replace me soon," Rosemarie says, reminding Frankie that her job at Falcone is temporary. "I'm counting on getting back into HR."

"Well, I hope you get what you want, but we'll miss you. At least I'll still get to see you, unless you kick me out when your first gigantic pay cheque arrives and you don't need a roommate anymore." Frankie smiles, but Rosemarie sees the doubt in his eyes.

The tea has gone cold and they're both tired. Rosemarie escorts Frankie to his new room and asks if he needs anything. Frankie says he's got everything he needs and he's just looking forward to sleeping in his new bed. "Goodnight, Rose. You've been a godsend to John, you know. To all of us, really."

After breakfast the next morning, Frankie goes to work while Rosemarie prepares to meet with Bernard. Finally, they've found the time to discuss Rosemarie's job prospects.

Rosemarie waits for Bernard at a café around the corner from her apartment. Bernard is late and Rosemarie wonders if he's forgotten. Just as Rosemarie contemplates leaving, Bernard rushes in. They order cappuccino and after a few minutes of small talk, Bernard fills Rosemarie in.

As it turns out, Bernard is only a silent partner. The parent company, Golden Daffodil Group, will handle reservations once they're up and running. They're sending a team up from Toronto to handle the local interviews for middle management positions. Bernard tells Rosemarie that she'll be hearing from them soon. Still, Rosemarie will have to ace her interview because Bernard says they're also looking to recruit from within the existing corporate structure.

"You're a shoo-in for that job, Princess."

"Can I use you for a reference?" Rosemarie asks.

"I already put a good word in for you," Bernard says. "Do you want a letter, too?"

Rosemarie figures Bernard's word must be worth its weight in footwear–while lighter than gold, Rosemarie's shoe collection is the most valuable asset she owns. "That would be very helpful," Rosemarie says.

"Why don't you write it, and I'll sign it," Bernard suggests.

"Okay. Although I don't know what to say about myself."

"Tell them you're the hottest thing to hit HR since... " Bernard pauses. He looks puzzled. "See. You better write it, Princess.

I'm no good at that sort of thing. Good luck with the interview," he says. Bernard is out the door before Rosemarie can thank him.

***

Since Rosemarie decided to take Frankie in as a roommate, she's been under a lot less pressure. Things are working out better than Rosemarie expected. She and Frankie have slipped into a comfortable routine and they're getting along like a couple of old spinsters. Even Rosemarie's best friend, Jen is astonished that it's working out so well. Jen confessed that she's a bit envious of Rosemarie's relationship with Frankie. Rosemarie feels guilty that she hasn't spent any time with Jen since she started working full time at Falcone. She hasn't had time for anything but work.

September flies by like a twister over Kansas. Rosemarie is able to make regular payments to her sister every payday. A couple more payments and she'll be back in the black.

It is almost the end of October when Rosemarie finally gets a call for an interview for the new hotel. Rosemarie is so optimistic, she's ready to celebrate. She asks Frankie what he's got planned for the weekend.

"Inventory. Didn't John tell you?" Frankie asks with concern. "It's our year-end and everyone has to work overtime. No exceptions. It's the one rule nobody dares to break."

"I have a vague recollection, now that you mention it. But it's Halloween, Frankie. I love Halloween! I was hoping we could get dressed up and go out with Jen."

"Yeah, well unless you want to go trick or treating in your

Falcone costume, you'll be sadly disappointed. If we're lucky, we'll make last call at the *Itai*."

"Jen's going to kill me, Frankie. We always go out together on Halloween, and the Italian Hall is definitely not her kind of place."

"Too many Italians?"

"Too many *greaseballs*. Besides, the whole point is to hit as many parties as we can. There are some great prizes to be won for best costume. Jen always does it up right. Last year she was the sexiest witch in town."

"That's a tough act to follow. What were you?"

"A pirate. It's not easy to do a female pirate, you know... it's *harrrd*," Rosemarie says, rolling her r's. "Shopping is nothing but looting and plundering, so we're kind of experts on the subject. And there are exceptions to the rules concerning hygiene, but we have to make up for it with profanity. My big line was, 'the next time we go out raping and pillaging, I want to do the raping,' but it didn't really fly. You need a big attitude to pull that one off."

"And balls... cannon balls," Frankie says, playing along. "Size matters."

"Arrrrr!"

So, no parties, no costumes and definitely no Jen. Just another night at the meat market. Rosemarie hopes this will be the last year-end she'll ever have to work through at the store.

Lina's Ruse

When John told Gord that Lina's psychiatrist thought it would be a good idea if she had a little more social interaction, Gord volunteered to go visit Lina after work. Gord misses their chats. He's been working for Lina since he was a teenager, part-time after school then full-time after graduation. Every day Gord drove Lina to the bank and then home. After Gord's wife left him, Gord was in a funk that Lina worked to pry him out of. Lina said that Gord would never get over his wife leaving him if he continued to believe his happiness was tied to his ex. Lina told Gord to "get a life," and he did, to a certain extent. He joined a bowling league and took a few evening classes. Every day Lina would give him the same advice. *You gotta make your own fun, Gordo.*

Gord taps on the open door and asks if this is a good time for a visit. Lina stares out the window from a chair in the corner of her room while the nurse administers her medication. The nurse is reluctant to leave. She instructs Gord to keep it short. "Mrs. Falcone is very tired and needs her rest." Before she can issue further warnings, the telephone at the nurses' station rings and she rushes off leaving the door propped open.

Gord uses the telephone's ring to deliver a greeting from The Electric Light Orchestra. *"Hello. How are you? Have you been alright, through all those lonely lonely lonely lonely—"*

Lina springs to life with more vigour than she's shown in years. "Quick! Shut the door," she whispers.

"Whoa, Lina. What's up?"

"Will you pipe down and shut the door, you eejit," Lina hisses. "I need to talk to you in private."

"Okay, okay. Relax, you're all uptight."

"Hand me that box of Kleenex, and keep your eye on the door." Lina spits something into the tissue, then reaches into her bra and pulls out another lumpy wad. She presses it into Gord's hand. "Get rid of these. Sell them if you can, I know you're connected."

Gord inspects the contents of the tissue and sees a fairly good sized pile of pills. They're all stuck together after spending enough time under Lina's tongue to melt the coating off and presumably, enough time to fool the staff into thinking they'd been swallowed. Judging by the number, Gord guesses Lina has been accumulating them for a good while now. "Lina! What are you doing?"

"Some kinda psychedelic drugs. They were making me crazy."

"I think you mean *psychotropic*, and they're supposed to help make you *not* crazy. And what I meant was, what are you doing getting rid of them?"

"I can't go into it right now. Nurse Ratchet could be back at any moment. All you need to know is that it's a ruse and I'm fine, as long as I can keep fooling them into thinking I'm taking them. When I found out they thought I wasn't, I adopted the slack-jaw-zombie look that's all the rage around here. It seems to have worked. They think I'm getting better *because* of the drugs. You have to help me, Gord," Lina pleads. "Who knows what they'll try next? They'll tie me down and give me an injection or maybe shock treatment."

"Holy Rocky Horror, Lina! I can't take these," Gord whispers. "Do you know what kinda trouble I'll be in if–"

Lina's countenance reverts to her drugged-zombie look, which indicates to Gord that the nurse has returned.

140

Gord pockets the wad. "Well, Lina, I can see you're tired, so I'll be going now. You be good and follow doctor's orders and you'll be feeling better in no time," he announces for the benefit of his audience. He tips his *Falcone* cap and squeezes past the nurse. She scowls at him. Lina is right, that woman is very scary looking. She could be Louise Fletcher's double.

His hands are shaking so much he can't roll a spliff. Gord is feeling a little paranoid himself now. *Connected.* As if. He only smokes medical grade marijuana; the stuff that's low THC, high CBD. Old school, nothing like the hydroponic street-grade weed they're growing nowadays. And even if there was a market for tranquillisers-with-previous-experience, the dude Gord buys from doesn't handle anything but cannabis.

Whenever Gord drove Lina home, she always gave Gord a "tip" as she called it; a little extra pocket money for service above and beyond the call of duty. Lina was unaware that John appointed Gord to be her bodyguard while she was carrying the company's bank deposit. Gord never acknowledged this fact to Lina, mostly because he didn't want her to feel diminished in any way. Lina isn't the sort of person who requires protection–she's the strongest woman Gord knows. Gord also appreciated the extra cash. Lina always seemed to have lots of it, and it helped to support his drug habit. It was a win-win situation and Gord never felt that he was taking advantage of Lina's generosity.

Gord doesn't know if he should go to John and tell him what he knows, or just flush the lot down the toilet. Maybe John won't believe him and he could end up getting Lina committed. If they think Lina is getting better because of these drugs, she must not need them, Gord figures. And if she doesn't need them, what the heck is she doing in there in the first place? Gord decides he can't handle this alone. He isn't family and nobody will listen to him.

Frankie slips into the walk-in cooler downstairs where Rosemarie is counting stock. She doesn't hear Frankie enter or sneak up behind her. "Trick or treat, smell my feet, give me something sweet to eat!"

"Jesus, Frankie. You'll give me a heart attack!"

"Sorry, doll. How's it going? Are you nearly finished in here? Everybody else is just about done. We'll have to hurry if we want to catch last call at the Italian Hall."

"Yeah, I've only got one more shelf to count and it's freezing in here."

"Hurry up and I'll walk over with you."

"Okay, okay. If you help me, we'll be finished before you can say *boo*. I can't reach the top shelf and I can't find the step stool. I think they took it upstairs. Is everybody going?"

"Yeah, mostly. Tracey and Carol never come, but a lot of the others have already started to make their way over there."

Frankie scrambles up the end of the shelving unit with the dexterity of a monkey. "Hey, doll face! I can see my house from here!"

"Be careful, Frankie. You're scaring me."

"Relax, I was born in the circus, remember? Okay, ready? I got two calabrese, one sopressa and hold on, *uno, due, tre, quattro, cinque, sei, sette...* and seven Genoa–four mild and three hot."

"Hold on, I can't find calabrese on my list."

"Look under *soppressata piquante*," Frankie tells Rosemarie just as Nick comes in carrying an armload of salamis.

"That's what I need," Nick says. "You got some hot calabrese up there, Frankie? We got too many *mild* upstairs. Here, put these back and send me down a couple hot ones."

Rosemarie is trying to keep up and correct the changing count. She's distracted watching the twins toss the giant salamis back and forth with practised precision, not unlike a real circus act. Nick throws the last one up, while Frankie throws one more down. The two oversized flattened sausages collide midair. Nick catches the one that was aimed at him, while the other pings off the edge of the shelf and hits the floor with a thud.

"Good thing it's wrapped," Rosemarie quips before she notices the gloom that envelopes the twins.

Frankie climbs down. He and his brother stand motionless. Slack-jawed, they both stare at the fallen meat product.

Nick breaks the spell. "Come on, Frankie," he says. "It's only a salami." Nick wraps his arm around his brother's shoulder, two halves of the same heart. Frankie and Nick walk away sullenly as if they've forgotten Rosemarie exists.

"Hey! Wait up." Rosemarie scrambles to catch up before they leave without her. The Italian Hall is only two blocks away but she doesn't want to walk alone at this late hour.

The *Itai* is jumping. A lot of people in the bar are dressed up but not in Halloween costumes. Most of the men are dressed in formal wear. Gord hands Rosemarie a beer while he sips a Coke. He tells Rosemarie that there's a wedding upstairs and a lot of guys came down to do shots of espresso before they drive home. He says the bride is the daughter of one of Falcone's suppliers and the bride's father has invited the staff to come upstairs for a drink. "Drink up, Rosie. Let's go shake a leg before the band calls it quits," Gord says.

Upstairs in the banquet hall, Rosemarie finds most of her co-workers huddled around the bar. John raises his glass to Rosemarie, then continues his conversation with Timo. Mervin is dancing with a couple of the cashiers and a group of bridesmaids. The twins stand together in silence over at the far end of the bar. Rosemarie wonders again what happened in the walk-in cooler to upset them so much.

Gord interrupts Rosemarie's thoughts to coax her onto the dance floor. He smells kind of skunky, like he just smoked up. As they join in to do the *Monster Mash*, Gord lets loose. Naturally, he knows all the words. When the song ends, Rosemarie tells Gord she's got to sit down. Rosemarie is wiped out and her feet are sore.

"Suit yourself, Rose," Gord says. Before Rosemarie makes it to an empty table at the back of the room, Gord has found another partner. He's giving her a whirl she won't soon forget.

A couple of cold beers appear in front of Rosemarie, courtesy of Timo. Timo and John have come to join Rosemarie and they sit down on either side of her. The father of the bride comes around to their table carrying a tray of shots. He tells them to relax and enjoy themselves. He claims he'll be handing out cigars next time they meet, so Rosemarie can't help but cast her eyes at the bride's belly.

Their host seems pleased. *At least he's not toting a shotgun*, Rosemarie thinks. John thanks the bride's father and apologizes for his staff taking over the party. "They've been working real hard and they're just letting off a bit of steam," John says.

Timo wastes no time. He helps himself to a shot and downs it in one go. Timo lines up three more and encourages John and Rosemarie to participate in his favourite hobby. "Bottoms up, kids!" Timo says.

The clear liquid burns as it makes its way down Rosemarie's throat. "What is this?" she chokes.

"Sambuca, sweet tits. Have another," Timo offers, and lines up three more.

Rosemarie feels quite revived now. She's getting her second wind. Rosemarie would rather dance with Timo than drink with him, even though she's out of her league on both counts. She remembers Timo ripping up the gymnasium floor in grade eleven at a Sadie Hawkins dance when Mandy Foster brought him as her date. Poor Mandy ended up sitting alone most of the night because so many of the other girls wanted their turn with the big mad Finlander with the crazy blue eyes. When the band strikes up a decent rendition of the Stone's *Respectable*, Rosemarie asks Timo if he wants to dance.

"Okay, but I'm gonna have to fuck you," Timo warns her. "'Cause as far as I'm concerned, dancing is foreplay."

Timo outshines Gord with his moves. He's shimmying and shakin' and riffin' along with *Keef.* They're both laughing and sweating and every girl in the room is jealous, maybe even the bride. Too soon the number is over, and the bandleader announces the last dance. The bride and groom take to the floor, followed by the wedding party and a few stragglers; all invited guests. Rosemarie suddenly feels seriously underdressed in her *Falcone* uniform. She left her apron and cap at the store, but she's still wearing a long sleeve red crew neck and jeans. She hears a familiar refrain and when the singer croons, *"Never seen you looking so lovely as I did tonight..."* Rosemarie bursts out laughing. She's the *Lady in Red!* Before Rosemarie can let Timo in on the joke, John slips up behind them and asks politely if he can cut in.

Timo refuses to relinquish his rights.

"Sorry, buddy. She's too hot for you," he says.

"That's okay, Mo. I gotta get going anyhow. Another big day tomorrow. You kids have a good time," John says diplomatically. John disappears while Rosemarie shamelessly lets Timo crotch rub his way through the last dance.

When the music ends and the band starts to take down their equipment, Rosemarie looks around for Frankie. It appears Frankie and Nick have left. Rosemarie is a little worried about walking home alone this late so she asks Timo for a ride.

"Sure, I'll take you home, but don't say I didn't warn you."

Frankie was in the bathroom and suddenly reappears. "I left my car at the store," he tells Rosemarie. Frankie flashes Timo a dirty look that puts a damper on any romantic ideas that either Timo or Rosemarie may have been harbouring. "I'll walk home with you, Rose," Frankie volunteers.

"Careful, Frankie. That chick is hot!" Timo licks his finger, touches Rosemarie's ass lightly then removes it quickly, hissing to dramatize he's been burned.

"You're a real gentleman," Frankie tells him.

"Oh, no, I'm not," Timo argues. "Adiós, my red Rose," Timo says salaciously. Like a gallant knight of questionable honour, Timo grabs Rosemarie's hand and kisses it. "See you both tomorrow, bright and early."

The night air is crisp. In spite of the cool temperature, Rosemarie and Frankie walk home at a leisurely pace, each lost in their own thoughts. Rosemarie is thinking about John. She wishes Timo would have stepped aside tonight. She likes Timo but there's no way she'd ever consider going out with him. John, on the other hand... Rosemarie is not exactly sure how she feels about him. Rosemarie is drawn to John in a way she can't explain. John certainly is handsome, although not like his cousins who share the boyish good looks often associated with athletes and movie stars. John's not a pretty boy. He's more *rugged*, which seems somehow incongruous with John's gentle personalty. Perhaps if John wasn't her boss Rosemarie might like to explore that aspect a little further. In the meantime, she'd like to explore any man a little further. Rosemarie hasn't had any sexual attention since Brian split, and tonight, Timo made her feel sexy again. In fact, she's quite aroused.

Rosemarie sneaks a quick glance over at Frankie. She wonders briefly if Frankie really is gay. And if he is, would converting a gay man, even for one night, benefit her ego? Would it make her feel more sexually powerful or would she end up hating herself for being devious and manipulative? Before Rosemarie can come to a conclusion, the short walk is over and they reach home.

Frankie says he's tired and goes to bed. Rosemarie is still wound up and knows she won't be able to get to sleep yet, so she goes upstairs and nestles in front of the gas fireplace in her favourite chair. She loves that chair. The mechanism that makes it rock and swivel is a marvel of engineering. It surprises everyone the first time they try it. It feels more like gliding than rocking. Its bucket shape is more suited to a tilt-a-whirl than an occasional chair, and the soft touch of the hot pink faux-suede upholstery creates a sensation that's unmistakably sexy.

Rosemarie rocks in the dark, lost in her libidinous thoughts. She hears Frankie's footsteps on the stairs.

Frankie sits down on the floor beside Rosemarie and says he can't sleep either. He sees Rosemarie rubbing her swollen feet and asks, "Are your dogs sore?"

"Yeah, what a night," Rosemarie says. "I probably shouldn't have given 'er so hard on the dance floor. We have to be back at the store first thing in the morning."

"Daylight Savings Time. We get an extra hour." Frankie takes Rosemarie's bare foot in his hands and gently massages the sole.

"Mmm, that's nice," Rosemarie moans softly as Frankie works the kinks out with his knuckles. "What happened tonight, Frankie? In the cooler, I mean."

"Oh, that. It's nothing really. It's just... well, that's how our mother died."

"She was hit with a salami?"

"No," he says. "Nothing that dramatic." Frankie involuntarily releases a strangled chortle when he realises how silly that sounds. "Our parents were acrobats in the circus you know, *aerialists*. They had a three-act with Uncle Giuseppe–he was the catcher and they were both flyers," Frankie says. His eyes sparkle in the flickering firelight as he recounts the tale he's heard a hundred times. He knows

149

every detail, as if he had witnessed the event himself.

"Some big shot scout was in the audience and they were trying to impress him. They were near the end of the performance–the grande finale. Giuseppe releases Francis–that's our dad–while Tessa flies off the swing and they cross in the air. Francis lands back on the swing and Giuseppe catches Tessa. It was their signature move. *The Flying Calabrese.* Except Giuseppe didn't catch her. Tessa collided with Francis midair and fell. It's not like they were working without a net–Tessa bounced off the edge, Lancaster style. She died instantly."

"Oh!" Rosemarie cries. She suddenly realises the significance. "Oh, no."

"Yeah. When that salami hit the floor, it was our mother lying there. Weird eh? Sorry about that."

"Oh, Frankie." Rosemarie grabs both his hands and sits forward. Her lips graze Frankie's ear. "I'm so sorry."

Frankie doesn't let go. He hangs on like she's a trapeze and he's working without a net. Rosemarie kisses Frankie softly on the forehead and feels his tension begin to dissolve. Frankie still doesn't let go. Instead, he pulls her down on top of himself.

A wave of heat sweeps over Rosemarie, igniting the passion she's been trying so hard to suppress. They kiss each other madly, all over. Kisses land wherever they can grab hold. Kissing leads to groping.

"You taste like licorice," Frankie whispers.

"*Liquorish*? Or just liquor?" Rosemarie asks, her breath coming in gasps. "I don't suppose you're packing latex?"

"In my room," Frankie pants. He lifts Rosemarie off the floor and cradles her like a fallen salami. He carries her downstairs.

"Shit! Fuck! Shit! Wake up, Frankie. What time is it?" Rosemarie shakes Frankie and jumps out of bed. She runs around his room picking up her clothes.

"Relax, Rose. It's Sunday. Come back to bed," Frankie yawns.

Rosemarie is hysterical now. "Year end!" she shouts, propelling Frankie out of bed and into action. "We're in big trouble!"

***

In spite of gaining an extra hour, they're still one short. By the time Rosemarie and Frankie reach the store they're more than an hour late. Everyone assumes they've overslept by re-setting their clocks in the wrong direction. Or, perhaps more likely, because they were out late partying like everyone else. Only John eyes them suspiciously and gives them a rather cool reception. "You're late," John says, stating the obvious.

"Sorry, cuz," Frankie apologizes. "Forgot to set the clock."

"Guess you share a clock, too," John says and leaves them feeling like a pair of guilty teenagers.

Rosemarie has a wicked headache. She's parched, in spite of how much she drank last night. Or because of it. Somehow Rosemarie manages to get through the morning without any more mishaps (like almost vomiting into the olive display when she unearthed some unidentified petrified food product. It was stuck to the bottom of the bin and Rosemarie had to bend over and reach in head first to extract the wayward item. While it remained unidentified, it was more putrid than petrified. The rancid smell overwhelmed her. Rosemarie only just made it to the bathroom before she retched up the sparse contents of her stomach).

A lot of the other members of staff silently share Rosemarie's pain through their own hangovers. Rosemarie wishes she could crawl under a counter and take a nap, maybe never wake up. Gord is the only one who appears to be none the worse for wear. That's because Gord doesn't drink and only sipped a Coke. And Timo looks chipper. Practise, Rosemarie supposes. Timo's an old hand at this sort of thing, *the bastard*.

The count is complete just before the store re-opens for business. Since Rosemarie is no longer scheduled for regular duty on the weekends, she's able to go home. Frankie is not so lucky and has to stay for the duration. Rosemarie will have a mountain of work to do tomorrow, pricing the inventory cost sheets and organizing documents for the accountants to prepare financial statements. For today, Rosemarie plans to take a long hot bath and try to catch up on her sleep.

Clean and dry two hours later, Rosemarie flops down on her bed. Late afternoon sunlight slants across her bedroom floor. Rosemarie dozes off and on, while flashes of last night's events keep her from getting any real sleep. Her memory is hazy with some serious lapses. Rosemarie realises she has behaved despicably, taking advantage of Frankie when he was at a low ebb. She regrets not being able to remember exactly what happened after the passionate whirl upstairs in front of the fire landed her in her own guestroom as a guest. Alcohol amnesia, Jen would call it. Another term comes to mind, but *slut* might be too harsh and it sounds so high school. Femme Fatale? Siren? Temptress? *Oh, my God. What have I done?* The real question is, will Frankie forgive her?

.

It takes Rosemarie a long time to look up the cost of goods on Falcone's suppliers' invoices. Time that she could spend sorting out the bookkeeping nightmare.

The accounting program Rosemarie downloaded seems easy enough to use. If she can get John's approval to purchase the program before the free trial expires, she could implement it in time for the first period-end of this new fiscal year. Rosemarie doesn't think she'll have trouble convincing John of its efficiency. Once the inventory is priced, she'll run a financial report to prove it to him.

Rosemarie compiles documents from the list Falcone's accountant faxed over. She finds statements from Canada Revenue Agency for HST and Source Deductions, indicating that both returns have been reported on time. She notes that the required reporting periods are to remain quarterly and monthly, respectively. When Rosemarie looks over the entries on the most recent HST return, she discovers that Lina did not deduct any input tax credits for HST paid on purchases and expenses.

Rosemarie locates the previous quarter's HST return in Lina's files and sees the error has been repeated. Lina has overpaid Canada Revenue. If they can deduct the unclaimed sum from future payments, this could be good news.

John could use some good news, Rosemarie thinks. She takes a break and grabs a cup of coffee. Rosemarie reflects on recent events and ponders John's sudden change in attitude, at least towards her. He can't be that upset over her being an hour late, can he? And the way John looked at her and Frankie when they finally did make it into work yesterday. He looked... mad? No. He looked *wounded.*

When Frankie came home from work last night, Rosemarie asked if they could talk about what happened between them. Turns out, Frankie regrets their late night tryst, too. He agreed that their friendship and household arrangement was too valuable to mess with. They both vowed to never let it happen again. What a relief. Rosemarie doesn't want Frankie to move out and she certainly doesn't want to worry about where the next rent payment is coming from. She needs him. Her other needs will have to be fulfilled by someone other than Frankie.

As if on cue, John walks in. "Hey," he says.

"Hey, yourself," she says. Rosemarie feels a little nervous around John, now. She has a strange sensation she can't pinpoint. Something has changed between them. Rosemarie suppresses the impulse to ask John about it. Instead, she aks, "Have you got a minute to take a look at this HST return? There's a very curious error you need to know about."

"Not another," John moans. "I don't think I can take anymore."

"No, this is a good one. At least I think so," Rosemarie

explains. "You might be getting some money back from the government." John brightens up, so Rosemarie continues. "Lina hasn't been claiming input tax credits on HST returns. I haven't looked back to see how long she's been failing to claim, and I'll have to double check with Canada Revenue Agency to find out how far back we can go, provided they will allow us to make a deduction from a future payment. They could end up owing you a lot of money."

"Wow. Good news, for once. It's very strange, though. Lina would never pay the government one extra cent in taxes. Maybe she really is losing it."

"Any news about your mom? I hear Gord went to visit her."

"Oh yeah, there's news alright, but it ain't good. Gord claims Lina hasn't been taking her meds, which is what I suspected when the doctor told me she should be improving. It's just that I don't know if I can believe Gord, you know? Lina seems to be doing so much better and if she hasn't been taking her medication... well, it just doesn't add up."

"Whatever the case is, it's good news she's getting better, right?"

"Yeah, it is, I guess." John doesn't look convinced. "Anyhow, Rose, I just stopped in to see if you need me for anything."

"Not really. For now, I'm making good progress here," she fibs, partly for John's benefit and partly because she doesn't know whether her news will be good or not. "And I've got another little surprise for you that I think you'll like."

"Later, Rose. I've had enough surprises for now and I gotta get going."

Rosemarie continues to plug away at the accountant's list and fill in the cost of goods on the inventory sheets. She goes home with the notion she has accomplished something.

Roseanna stops by Rosemarie's apartment after supper for a visit. She conveys the usual news of their mother's complaints concerning the casino "stealing" her pension, and a bit of yammering about not seeing Rosemarie in weeks.

Rosemarie and Roseanna take their tea upstairs to watch the first snowflakes of the season descend. Smatterings of white powder stick to the rooftops and accumulate on the slanted surface of the windows. They sit in comfortable silence, unaware of the usual city noises, now hushed under a layer of snow. For now, they welcome the snow as it hails the change of seasons. Soon, they'll hate the stuff. When they have to trudge through it, or shovel it. Or worse, when it melts and everything turns grey and they're forced to wade through slush that leaves nasty salt stains on boots.

"Did I tell you Billie passed her junior bronze?" Roseanna asks.

"Wow. That was fast. Didn't she just start figure skating last year?"

"Yeah, her coach says she's a natural. Which is great, 'cause she's too small for hockey."

"Bet that won't last," Rosemarie says. Billie is Roseanna's youngest daughter. Rosemarie recalls how rapidly the other three girls developed in the wake of their recent growth spurts.

"Late bloomer, I guess. Anyhow, they changed the age categories this year so she qualifies for Sectionals. Used to be that girls had to be under the age of twelve before July first to qualify. But they split juvenile into two categories now: under eleven, and under fourteen, so she's not too old to compete at Northerns.

"Now she's hounding me to make her a new costume to dazzle the judges. Billie figures she can make it all the way to Junior Nationals before she turns fourteen. Imagine that! Jeez, Mare, I can barely hem their jeans and now I gotta be a costume designer, too. I haven't a clue where to start. All her skating dresses have been hand-me-downs from other skaters, up to now. Too bad she can't wear her sisters' cast offs. Wouldn't do to have her twirling around in their old stuff, though. They all have big numbers printed on the back."

Rosemarie giggles and says, "Quit complaining, at least you got one girly-girl."

"Who you callin' a girly-girl?" Frankie's voice chirps up from downstairs. "Is that your sister? Can I come up?" he asks.

Roseanna and Frankie finally meet. "Charmed, I'm sure," Roseanna says like some kind of southern belle when Rosemarie introduces them. "My youngest is a girly-girl," Roseanna confesses like she's ashamed. "I was just bitching about having to make her a figure skating outfit."

"Do you sew?" Frankie asks.

"A bit, but not up to the standard required for this project. And get this, she wants it to look sexy. Can you believe it? She's thirteen and she wants–correction... make that, *needs* it to be sexy! She says she hasn't got a chance of winning otherwise."

"Sounds like you've got your hands full there. Too bad my aunt isn't up to it. She used to make some killer costumes."

Rosemarie brings Roseanna up to speed regarding the family circus, while Frankie goes to fetch himself a cup of tea.

When Frankie comes back up upstairs he asks Roseanna how big her daughter is. Rosemarie and Roseanna are the same height as each other. In the same silly way she used to tell grown-ups how old she was, Rosemarie claims they're *five-foot-three going on five-foot-four*. Except for Billie, Roseanna's daughters are taller than both her and Rosemarie now. The three older girls take after their father, Eddie, who is lean and lanky.

"Smaller than average," Roseanna tells Frankie. "She weighs less than Eddy's old dog and only comes up to here." Roseanna stands up and holds her hand out just below her chin to indicate Billie's height. "Why?"

"I was thinking maybe you could copy one of Tessa's old costumes. Maybe make a pattern or whatever."

"No way, Frankie," Rosemarie protests. "You said Lina would kill you if you ever touched that trunk again."

"Oh, relax, Rose. That was a million years ago. Besides, she won't know as long as we put it back where we find it."

"Frankie! You're a saviour," Roseanna says. If it looks like it'll fit I could get Billie to try it on. Then I can trace it to make a pattern. And I'll make sure she's squeaky clean. Your aunt will never know it's been gone, much less touched."

Rosemarie has an odd, almost portentous feeling, a sense of foreboding, but Frankie assures her it will be fine. Rosemarie tries to shake the sensation while the three of them pull their coats and boots on. They pile into Frankie's little car and he drives them over to his old house.

"What if Nick's around?" Rosemarie asks. She imagines Nick might not agree with Frankie's generous offer.

"Relax. Nick's at work and we'll only be a couple minutes. I know exactly where they are."

Both women are surprised to see such a clean and tidy household. "You'd never know the occupants are a couple of bachelors," Rosemarie marvels.

"Only one on this side now, and maybe not for long," Frankie corrects her, reminding Rosemarie about Nick's impending marriage proposal.

John still lives with his mother on the other side of the duplex. A central staircase literally divides the house in half. Two narrow stairwells meet at the top landing where French doors enclose the attic. The doors are locked, so Frankie takes the other stairs down to Lina's bedroom and returns in a moment with her keys.

When they enter the cramped space Rosemarie and Roseanna are impressed. Lina's sanctuary and Rosemarie's apartment share a similar view. This one is a few blocks back and higher up the hills surrounding the harbour. It's only slightly less spectacular. Beneath the window a wall seat nestles in the dormer. Three-quarter walls meet the sloped ceiling that follows the contour of the roof and gives the room that cozy feeling associated with secret hideouts and surreptitious plots.

"You can see why she spent so much time up here," Frankie says. "Great view, eh?"

Frankie wastes no time finding the right key on Lina's key chain. He opens the old steamer trunk with a flourish and pulls out a tissue-wrapped bundle. The trunk is jam-packed. While Frankie and Roseanna unwrap and inspect the first item, Rosemarie snoops around and pokes a little deeper into the trunk.

"Wow! Hubba, hubba. Would you get a load of this!" Roseanna exalts.

"Do you think it'll fit your daughter?" Frankie asks.

"She can't fill the cups, thank God. Wow, Frankie, your mom wore this?" Roseanna holds up a glittering gold garment with wide-set straps encrusted with a string of fake rubies. The gems encircle what appear to be at least double D's. Another string of jewels circle the hips and hold down a scalloped bit of lace that makes an excuse for a skirt.

"Pretty sexy, eh? That's the last one she wore. According to Lina, Tessa was spilling out of it after we were born."

"Probably leaking, too. What else you got in your bag of tricks?"

"How about this one," Frankie says, shaking out a much tamer outfit. "This one was strictly for practice," he says. It's only slightly less stunning. Black and white zebra-striped silk forms two cups of the halter that plunges into a deep "v" where two rows of tiny buttons covered in black silk promenade side by side down the white satin bodice. A double layer of black and white striped ruffles flounce around the hips.

"It's perfect. Believe me, Frankie. I'll have it back to you before you can say flying camel sit spin."

"Okay. Take it and let's go," Rosemarie says. She returns the rejected costume to its nest and snaps the lid of the trunk shut. "We really shouldn't be in here."

Rosemarie doesn't need to tell them twice. Roseanna and Frankie scurry down the stairs yakking like a couple of delirious stage-mothers. Frankie tells Roseanna that he follows figure skating and watches whenever it comes on TV or when there's an ice show at the Fort William Gardens. He has about a million questions for Roseanna.

Rosemarie notices Frankie forgot to lock the trunk and the attic door. She follows them down the stairs and out of the house, but says nothing about it. Her mind is reeling. Her premonition was accurate.

After her call is transferred twice, Rosemarie waits on hold for so long, she begins to wonder if she's been cut off. She is finally put through to someone at Canada Revenue Agency who should be able to answer her questions about HST returns. A recorded voice instructs Rosemarie to leave a message stating her name, the company's business number and purpose of her call.

It seems nobody answers their phones anymore. They're either screening calls so they're better prepared, or simply hiding behind the brick wall of voice mail. Rosemarie admits to having done this herself on occasion when a persistent caller became too persistent. At the board, she sometimes vetted calls from people who tried to influence her hiring decisions. Applicants often refused to adhere to her instructions: *don't call us, we'll call you.*

When someone from CRA returns Rosemarie's call, the person identifies herself as an auditor. This causes Rosemarie to assume there has been some confusion and that her message has been misunderstood.

"No, there's no mistake, Ms Catanzaro," the auditor says.

"We've been trying to reach a representative of your company for quite some time now. We've failed to receive any response to date. According to my records, it's been more than four months since our initial correspondence."

Rosemarie's the one who's confused now. She has caught up with the backlog of filing and she isn't aware of any such correspondence. Rosemarie apologizes. "I'm sorry, Ms ... what did you say your name was?"

"Christine Constantine."

"I'm new here, Ms Constantine. I'm temporarily replacing the regular bookkeeper who is on sick leave. I haven't seen this letter you're referring to."

"*Letters*. Plural. We've sent several."

"I'm sorry, Ms—"

"Call me Christine."

"Okay, Christine. I'm afraid I don't know what you're talking about. I was calling about a mistake on an HST return."

This seems to satisfy the auditor. She puts Rosemarie on hold while she looks up a copy of the ostensibly missing letter.

Once Rosemarie has heard what Christine Constantine tells her, she's pretty sure John is not going to think this is good news. This sort of thing rarely is. According to CRA's initial correspondence, the company had been randomly selected for an audit. When they didn't hear from the client, they went ahead and scheduled it to commence the second week in November.

"Next week?" Rosemarie almost shouts into the receiver.

"Yes, that's correct. Is there a problem?"

"It's just that it's our year-end, and as I said, the bookkeeper has been off sick. We're really far behind here. Is there any way we can reschedule?" Rosemarie asks as nonchalantly as her panic will allow.

Christine says she'll see what she can do and promises to get back to her. Judging by the tone of her voice, Rosemarie gets the impression she may be disinclined to grant any leniency. Definitely not good news.

***

It's John's turn for confusion. He rubs his temples and asks Rosemarie the same questions she asked the auditor.

"That's right," Rosemarie confirms. "Next week. I tried to buy us some time but it doesn't look promising."

"It's just that with Lina gone, I don't know if I can handle this right now," John laments. "She really was the glue around here."

Speaking of sticky... Rosemarie might as well keep going. It's time she shared her suspicions with the manager of this outfit, even if he is Lina's son. "There's more, John. This might come as a shock to you, and it might take a while. Can we talk after work tonight?"

"Yeah, sure. I'd appreciate any input you have, Rose, I'm gonna need all the help I can get."

"If you don't mind, I could come back in later this evening, after the store closes," Rosemarie suggests. The store closes at eight o'clock now that summer is over. She doesn't want anyone to overhear what she has to tell John.

"Actually, that would be better for me, too. That'll give me time to look after some other stuff first. They should be finished cleaning by nine-thirty," John says. "Come to the receiving door and ring the buzzer if the door is locked."

"All right, John. I'll see you back here in the office at ten o'clock tonight."

At quarter to ten, Rosemarie asks Frankie if she can borrow his car to run over to the drug store to pick up a few things.

"Sure." Frankie tosses her the keys. "Shoppers is open 'till midnight. Could you pick up some milk while you're out? Either that, or you'll have to pour vodka on your Cheerios in the morning."

A gentle reminder that Rosemarie finished the last carton without replacing it? Or a dig about excessive drinking? She's getting paranoid. It's probably just a joke. "Anything else we need?" Rosemarie asks casually. She doesn't want to arouse any suspicion.

"Not that I can think of," Frankie says. "I'll leave the hall light on in case you're not back before I go to bed."

The store appears deserted. The parking lot is empty except for John's truck parked near the loading dock. Rosemarie rings the buzzer and the receiving door swings open. "Come on in," John says. "I'll be with you in a sec. Nick and Mervin seemed to be taking forever, so I sent them home and told them I'd finish up." John coils the spray hose and snugs it into the wall bracket. "I thought it would be better if they didn't have any reason to talk," he says.

"Good thinking," Rosemarie agrees. "Which reminds me, Frankie asked me to bring home some milk when I told him I was going to the drug store. I even borrowed his car so he wouldn't be suspicious." She laughs at her own folly. "I better go grab a litre from up front or I'll blow our cover," Rosemarie says. She's embarrassed to admit what this must look like.

A few minutes later they're settled in on either side of Lina's desk. Rosemarie is seated in the position of power behind the desk, a little trick she learned early in her career.

"I don't know where to start so I'll just come out with it, John. After finding too many bookkeeping discrepancies to be a coincidence, I have come to the conclusion that Lina has been taking cash." *Stealing* seems too strong of a word, and she's careful to refer to the culprit by name, rather than saying, "your mother." Rosemarie rehearsed this in her head all evening.

John doesn't respond while he processes this information.

"Believe me, John, I wish I was wrong. I waited until I was absolutely sure."

He still doesn't respond. Rosemarie waits for the news to sink in. She waits and listens to the clock tick. Finally, John says, "I should have known."

"How could you, John?" Rosemarie sympathizes. "It wasn't that obvious. If I didn't go sticking my nose into places it probably doesn't belong, I would never have figured it out."

"No, really. I should have known," John says. "We never declare much of a profit. I'm careful with mark-ups and you can see for yourself this place is busy. And nobody is making huge wages. None of us are complaining because we've been sinking the profits back into the store. Lina always said that was a *good* thing 'cause we're building equity. And to her, it meant we hardly paid any corporate tax. Trouble is, we can't write off capital expenditures, so she's always on me when I want to buy new equipment. Takes forever to amortize, she says. How did she do it?"

"Well, to begin with, I think she sold stuff without a receipt. Probably for exactly the reason you just said; she didn't like paying taxes. That's an attitude she shares with a lot of your customers, I suspect. Then, when she got away with it, I think she wrote-off products that she'd actually sold and made an adjustment to the ledger." *Eighty-sixed it.* The irony writ large now that Rosemarie knows it was Lina who made up the code. "Now you know why I was so surprised when she failed to claim input tax credits," Rosemarie says.

John looks perplexed. "Yeah, that's still bugging me." John mulls over this bit of the puzzle. "What was the good news?" he asks.

"Good news?"

"Yeah, you mentioned something earlier about a surprise. You said I'd like it."

"Oh, that. I almost forgot about that," Rosemarie says. Her enthusiasm for implementing a computer program has been greatly diminished in light of her recent discovery. "I downloaded a trial version of a computer accounting program that I think will improve efficiency. I wanted to talk to you about purchasing the software. I've input most of the data from the ledger and thought if we... " Rosemarie's voice trails off when she sees that John is no longer paying attention. *He's tuned out*, she thinks. *He doesn't want to hear about this right now.* "John, I'm sorry. I know we have more important—"

John gets that *Eureka!* look on his face. "That's why she didn't want to computerize!"

"Because she wouldn't be able to cover her tracks!" Rosemarie concurs. She remembers how difficult it was to unearth Lina's buried treasure.

They both display a levity that's inappropriate under the circumstances. They're thrilled to have solved a piece of the puzzle. The gravity of the situation brings her back down with a sobering thought.

"Your mom must have known about the audit."

"Yeah. No wonder she went off the deep end," John says with more empathy than one would expect from a man who just found out his schizophrenic mother has been lying, cheating and stealing. "She must have been under a lot of stress."

John excuses himself. He says he's just going to run out to his truck for a minute. He grabs two coffee mugs on his way past the staff lunch room and returns carrying a bottle of wine.

"Sorry we don't have any good crystal," John says. He twists off the cap and fills the mugs. "This stuff's cheap and cheerful, but it'll do the job. *Salute!*"

"What are we toasting?"

"A new era!" John declares.

To Rosemarie's astonishment, John agrees that a computerized accounting program is just what they need. He encourages Rosemarie to let him know if she has any other ideas for improving efficiency. Rosemarie is bewildered. *Doesn't he even care about the money or what she did with it?* Instead of being emotionally exhausted, John talks about the future with enthusiasm. *Could it be that he's glad to be rid of Lina?* Either way, Rosemarie is enjoying John's company. It's great to see him in such a good mood again.

"What are you grinning at?" John asks.

171

"Oh, I'm just glad you're so amicable," Rosemarie slurs. "I mean, amenable."

"I love it when you talk like that."

Perhaps it's the wine talking. They drank most of the bottle and Rosemarie has a nice buzz going. "Like I'm drunk?" she giggles.

"No, big words like that." John leans back in one of those solid oak banker's chairs that are rarely seen in modern offices and prevalent in the basement offices of mom and pop establishments. Rosemarie can tell by John's practised precision that he knows exactly how far he can tilt before he springs back up. John rolls around to the other side of the desk and leans all the way back. He looks up into Rosemarie's face. "You're so smart."

Not smart enough to figure out what's making him so happy. Rosemarie watches John watching her with big puppy-dog eyes. John spins around to face Rosemarie. It looks like he's going to say something profound. "I like your hair," he says instead.

"Thanks. Frankie cut it," Rosemarie says, thrilled that John noticed.

At that, John's demeanor turns serious. "Frankie's a lucky dog."

Rosemarie is not sure if that means John is envious of his cousin's abilities, or their friendship. He might even be talking about their living arrangement. "We're just friends," Rosemarie reassures him.

"Doesn't look that way."

This looks more like jealousy than envy to Rosemarie. It causes her temperature to rise and brings a high colour to her cheeks. "I should go," she says. Rosemarie hands John her empty mug.

John reaches out to take the mug and wraps his hands around hers. "Don't go," he pleads.

John's plea rivets Rosemarie to the spot. The temperature in the room has shot up several degrees. Her heart races while she waits for whatever might come next.

"I never get you to myself," John complains. "Everybody wants you."

As shocking as this is to Rosemarie, there's no mistaking John's intentions now. She welcomes the affection. Slowly, Rosemarie pries John's fingers away one at a time, releasing his grip on the empty mug. She sets it down on the desk while their eyes remain locked. She can't release the grip he has on her. Rosemarie loses herself in John's gaze.

John kisses her, tentatively. His lips taste of wine. Unlike the cheap Chianti they drank, it's as if Rosemarie's palate has been cleansed and it's a fine old vintage she's appraising. He kisses her again softly. John tells Rosemarie that he's been wanting to do that since grade six. Before Rosemarie can say anything, he kisses her again, preventing further conversation. John explores the inside of Rosemarie's mouth with his tongue, slowly at first, allowing the pressure to build until neither of them are capable of keeping it bottled up a moment longer.

John sweeps the contents of the desk onto the floor, shattering the mugs and Rosemarie's resistance. He eases Rosemarie onto the desk and fumbles with the buttons on her shirt. She rips it open, sending the last couple of buttons flying. John covers Rosemarie in kisses, starting at her collarbone and working his way down... He skilfully unhooks Rosemarie's bra. She wriggles out of it like a snake shedding her skin. A small gasp escapes when John's mouth clamps onto her nipple. They fumble with jeans and zippers until all barriers are removed. No time to shut off lights. No time to find somewhere else to go. Their need is too urgent.

John's smooth olive skin smells of fresh soap and something else wholesome that Rosemarie can't name. He slides easily into her. He's hard and she's ready. The fit is perfect, like an old pair of jeans. Rosemarie can't hear what John is saying over the panting. The pounding of her own heart muffles the pounding the desk is taking. It's over too soon and their spent bodies lay motionless while their minds soar. Wearing nothing but socks, they are fully exposed under the glare of florescent lights, yet neither of them are ashamed of their nakedness. The truth has been exposed and it's exhilarating.

When Rosemarie catches her breath and regains her composure, she asks John what he was saying.

"Just that I wanted to do *that* since grade eleven."

"Johnny Falcone! You are full of surprises! You certainly never let on," Rosemarie scolds him. She strokes the stubble on his perpetual five o'clock shadow with the back of her hand.

John nibbles at Rosemarie's earlobe. "Why do you think I left the *Itai* so suddenly last Saturday?" he mumbles. "I couldn't stand to watch. It reminded me of that dance in high school when I got stuck with Selina DeMarco and you were dancing with Timo all night."

"*Slutina*! I haven't seen her in years. I forgot she asked you to Sadie Hawkins night. And for the record, I wasn't the only one dancing with Timo that night." Rosemarie pushes up to a sitting position to check to see if John is serious. "Why didn't you ask me to dance and rescue me from... oh, what's his name? That geek I came with. The one with the big thick glasses."

"I was too afraid you'd turn me down. And I'll have you know, that geek went on to become a very successful professional. I heard he's a chartered accountant."

"What *was* that guy's–"

John interrupts Rosemarie with a wet kiss. He leans back on the desk and smiles at her, his teeth sparkle to match the sparkle in his eyes. He gently strokes her hair.

Rosemarie doesn't know how to respond. She had no idea John had a crush on her. It's so thrilling, she doesn't want to spoil the moment. John continues to stroke Rosemarie's hair and trails his hand down her back until it comes to rest on her bum. He gives her a playful spank and she swats his hand away. "I better get dressed and get out of here before I get fired. There's no playing 'hide the sausage' on Falcone time, you know."

Rosemarie looks around to find where her clothes have fallen. She's momentarily shamed by the memory of another recent encounter. "I really have to get home," she says. The serious look on her face tells John she means it.

Reluctantly, John pulls on his underwear. "I'll clean up this mess," he says. He pulls her close for another lingering kiss.

When they're both put back together as best they can, John walks Rosemarie out to Frankie's car. He holds her hand and acts very shy again, like the teenage version of himself. He leans in for one more kiss which prevents Rosemarie from closing the car door. "I'm sorry we never did this sooner," he says. "And I can't wait to do it again." John steals one more kiss before Rosemarie can close the door.

He watches her through the window. John doesn't seem to be aware that it's cold out. He's not even wearing a jacket. Rosemarie rolls down the window and John takes advantage of the opening. He plants another quick kiss on Rosemarie's lips. "We'll talk tomorrow, John. Goodnight." Rosemarie rolls up the window.

John's hand is on his heart. Rosemarie doesn't hear him whisper, *"Buona notte, cuore mio."*

***

Across Connie Street in the staff parking lot, Timo waits in his truck. Mervin sits beside him. They're waiting for John and Frankie to leave the store. When John sent Nick and Mervin home early, Mervin had to walk around the block several times until Timo arrived.

They perk up when they see John come out with a woman. They watch her climb into Frankie's car. Timo strains his eyes to get a better look.

"Well, looky here," Timo says.

"Isn't that Miss... "

"Catanzaro."

"Oh, look, Timo. They're kissing. Isn't that sweet?"

"It's about time," Timo says. "I wondered when they'd get around to it."

"Are we still gonna butcher your bear, Timo?"

"Fuckin' right. I didn't sit out here all this time freezing my balls off only to put this fella back into the freezer. Conditions are perfect. He's nearly thawed."

Timo's buddy shot the bear at the dump last summer. He

kept it in his freezer and offered to pay Timo cash for his professional services. The problem was where to do the job. The health inspector would go nuts if he thought Falcone was handling wild meat. Unlike the "wild" boars which are actually raised in captivity and fed Tuscan grapes to give the meat an authentic flavour, a garbage-fed dump bear hung in Falcone's cooler would surely land them in deep shit. So Timo borrowed Nick's keys under the pretense that he wanted to do some knife sharpening. He kept the bear in the back of his truck under a tarp in the shade all afternoon so it would thaw by the time the store closed.

"I hope we can get started soon," Mervin says. "I still have to get over to the funeral home. I'm working the graveyard shift."

Besides working part-time at Falcone, Mervin is apprenticing to become a mortician. John told Mervin not to tell anyone because he was afraid customers might not like the idea of a mortician handling their food. When Giuseppe died, Lina wouldn't even shake hands with the funeral director. She said it had nothing to do with superstition. "When you handle food, you don't touch the undertaker," Lina declared. "Why do you think they wear gloves?"

"Don't worry, Merv," Timo says. "You can leave as soon as we unload this big lug. I won't need you once I start cutting."

Ever since Mervin started his apprenticeship at the funeral home, he's waited for an opportunity like this. His boss told him a skinned bear looks just like a human. "I just want to get a look at the body," Mervin says.

"And I just wanna get paid," Timo replies.

As promised, Frankie left the hall light on. Rosemarie manages to sneak in without facing him.

The next morning, Frankie is very quiet. He studies Rosemarie as she rushes around the kitchen. Rosemarie pours some cereal into a bowl and searches through the fridge only to discover she didn't bring the milk home. "Oops, must have forgot," she says. Rosemarie turns away from Frankie just in time to hide her reddening cheeks, a natural consequence as she recalls the reason.

It's Frankie's day off so Rosemarie asks him what he has planned.

"A few errands and some tests that are required for admission to Master Locks Academy of Hair Design."

"That's great, Frankie!" Rosemarie says. She's been encouraging Frankie to follow his dream of becoming a hair stylist so she's delighted he's decided to take a step in that direction. "Good luck," Rosemarie says referring to the tests. She grabs her coat and keys, and hurries down the stairs before Frankie can notice her new crimson blush.

When Rosemarie gets to the store, she doesn't pause upstairs to talk to any of the staff. She sits down at the desk to collect her thoughts and reflect on last night's encounter while she sips a cup of coffee. *Wow. That was something!* She can't believe it happened. She looks around and sees that John has cleaned up the mess they made. He has removed all evidence and the desk doesn't divulge its secrets. Rosemarie begins to sort through the tidy stack of papers when John comes in holding a mug. "Coffee," he says with a sly grin. "Morning, Rose. How are you?"

"Fine. Well, okay. How are you?" she stammers. She feels self conscious.

"Better than fine," John says. He's beaming. He hands her a button. "I guess I kinda got carried away and I apologize for that. I hope you're not mad at me."

"Of course not, John. That was... *nice*," Rosemarie says, not sure how to phrase it. Rosemarie doesn't want to get into a discussion about it right now. Anyone might hear them and John could be called away at any moment. "Can we talk about it later?" she asks.

"Sure. It's just... well, I want you to know that I'm not like that, you know. I mean, not normally. I just want you to know you're... *special*," he whispers.

Rosemarie blushes. She remains silent while Gord pushes a loaded two-wheel dolly past the open door. Rosemarie is so unsure of what to say. "You too," she mouths instead. With great effort and much louder than is required, Rosemarie announces that she needs to get started on the books. She needs to focus on the huge task that awaits her.

"I'll have a report to show you as soon as I finish inputting the data. I think you'll like what you see."

"I already do," John says, peeking over the rim of his coffee mug with those bedroom eyes Rosemarie can barely resist. "I gotta get upstairs. We'll talk later, okay?" John sneaks a quick look around then blows her a kiss.

He returns in a moment holding up a litre of milk. "You forgot this last night. "I'll put it back in the fridge," John says and disappears again.

Rosemarie forgot more than the milk last night. She forgot about propriety. She cast aside any semblance of correct or appropriate behaviour, never mind safety! It didn't even occur to her until she went to bed and recounted the experience that she'd had unprotected sex. With her boss, no less! Jesus, she's losing it. *But it was grand, wasn't it? He's so good looking, so caring and attentive, so... dreamy,* Rosemarie can't think straight. *Snap out of it,* she admonishes herself. *Get a grip!*

Rosemarie enters the figures from their year-end closing-balances as opening-balances in the new program. After a few hours of intense concentration, she's able to produce a clear picture of Falcone's fiscal position. It doesn't look too bad. Now that Lina isn't able to "take" any more cash, Rosemarie suspects it will look even better in the future. Rosemarie is pleased with the way the program handles reporting so she prints a few other reports as examples of its capability. There are only a few glitches to work out. She fiddles with the printer until she finally gets it formatted correctly, and she figures out how to set up the accounts payable by due date. Rosemarie adds the pro forma invoice for the software to the payables in anticipation of its approval. She can always reverse the entry by issuing a credit if she has to. The one thing Rosemarie can't do is a one-sided entry, which is good. Especially with bookkeepers like Lina at large.

When Rosemarie gets a phone call from Christine at Canada Revenue Agency, she isn't surprised that they've refused to reschedule. So she files all the documents that pertain to Falcone's last fiscal year-end in a banker's box to be delivered to the accountants once the auditor releases them. Rosemarie just hopes that nobody will be as interested as she was to follow the convoluted trail of Lina's entries. She'll have to bluff her way through any sticky questions. After all, this did happen *pre-Rosemarie,* and just like at the McTavish, Rosemarie is comfortable not taking responsibility for things she had no control over.

Rosemarie's work day is nearly over. As she prepares to go home, John enters the office. "Oh, good," she says. "I'm glad you're still here. I've got something to show you," she tells him.

"I can't wait," John says flirtatiously.

"No, really, John. Here, take a look at this." Rosemarie hands him the reports.

John sits back with the same ease he displayed last night. He scours the pages while he leans dangerously far back in his chair. John springs back up and says, "Doesn't look too bad. You're amazing, Rose."

"Yeah. And imagine how much better it'll be now that we know... "

"That's the only thing that's still bugging me, Rose. Where did the money go? I mean, Lina's never been a big spender. What the heck did she do with the money?" John asks.

"I have an idea."

"Oh, ya? Tell me."

"If you can spare a few minutes, I think it would be better to show you," Rosemarie says. "Come with me."

Rosemarie is careful to make sure Nick has arrived at work and won't be home. John follows Rosemarie out to the parking lot and watches Rosemarie climb into the passenger seat of his truck. John takes his seat behind the wheel and asks, "Where to?"

"Your place."

John grins. He raises his eyebrows in hopeful wonder.

"Just drive, Falcone," she ripostes.

When they arrive in front of John's house a few minutes later, Rosemarie does a quick check for Frankie's car. The coast is clear. John fiddles with the keys and eventually opens the front door. Rosemarie squeezes past him. "What's going on, Rose? What's with all the mystery?"

The interior layout is a mirror image of the other side of the duplex house. Rosemarie ignores John's questions and bolts up the stairs to the attic. John hurries to keep up as Rosemarie takes the stairs two at a time. Rosemarie pushes open the door that is normally locked. "That's strange," John mutters. Rosemarie throws open the lid of the trunk that's also normally locked.

"It's full of cash, John. Look!"

"What the heck? How did you—?"

"Long story. Short version is that Frankie loaned one of his mother's costumes to my sister and I accidentally discovered what I believe to be Lina's stash."

John pauses while he processes this shocking discovery. "Holy cow."

"Yeah. I have no idea how much there is, but here," she says pulling out one of many grocery bags stuffed with rolls of bills. "You can see your yourself... it's a lot."

"Holy cow," John repeats like a sound loop of a broken record. "I had no idea."

"Well, that's the point, isn't it? The thing is, we gotta get it out of here, John. When I saw the money, I closed the trunk before Frankie could see it. He was so busy chatting with my sister that he left with Lina's keys and forgot to lock up. But he's going to put that costume back where he found it and he's bound to see this!"

"What should we do?"

"We gotta get it out of here. Can we take it to the office and put it in the safe?"

"Good thinking, Rose."

"C'mon, John. Give me a hand, and for God's sake, hurry up! It's Frankie's day off and my sister promised to return that costume as soon as she's done. He could show up any minute!"

They both struggle to carry as many bags as they can down to John's truck. It takes them two trips. As John backs out of the driveway, Rosemarie spots Frankie's car headed towards them. She ducks down. As they pass, the cousins acknowledge each other with a toot of their horns. Looking in his rearview mirror, John watches Frankie pull into the driveway. He sighs with relief. "That was close."

Rosemarie imagines her excitement is similar to the adrenaline rush a gun moll gets while her gangster boyfriend drives getaway. She stays put until John confirms they're out of sight. When Rosemarie returns to a seated position beside John, she asks, "How can we get this into the office without anyone noticing?"

"I've got an idea," John says. He pulls over to the curb a block away from the store. "Give me a few minutes. Then you go around through the main entrance and tell the cashiers you forgot something in the office. I'll meet you down there."

"Shall we synchronize our watches?" Rosemarie jokes. She jumps out of the truck before anyone can see them arrive together.

John backs up to the loading dock and picks up a few empty cardboard boxes. He fills them with bags of money. He puts the boxes on the loading dock and, finding the receiving area deserted, loads the cartons onto the conveyor belt. John hits the button to send them downstairs. The day shift is over and it's not uncommon to see John perform Gord's duties after hours. Downstairs, John grabs the boxes off the belt and shuttles them into the office undetected. Rosemarie strolls in moments later and John tells her to shut the door. There's no lock on it, but everyone knows the unwritten rule that forbids anyone from entering when the office door is closed: *Knock and wait.*

They discuss what they should do, although neither of them have any idea how to proceed. With the audit scheduled to begin next week, John says he needs time to think about it. Rosemarie leaves John counting the money and goes home. She was curious about how much money was in Lina's stash but didn't think she should stick around any longer. They were so preoccupied with their caper, they didn't even talk about what happened between them last night.

When Rosemarie gets home, Frankie tells her that Roseanna stopped by to return Tessa's costume. "She can't wait to show you the copy she's making," he says. "And don't worry, I put the original right back where we found it and I returned Lina's keys. She'll never know anyone was in that trunk," Frankie reassures her. *I doubt that,* Rosemarie thinks. She's happy to let the issue drop.

***

Rosemarie and John were both so busy handling one catastrophe after another that they never found a moment to talk in private all week, although they exchanged meaningless glances whenever they met at the store. Even if she could have found an opportunity for a quick chat, Rosemarie didn't feel comfortable asking John how much money they discovered in the trunk so she didn't inquire. Strange as it seems, Rosemarie doesn't believe it's any of her concern. She's stuck her nose into the Falcone family's business enough already. What Rosemarie would like to discuss with John is their... she doesn't even know what to call it. It certainly wasn't a date. Every other term she comes up with sounds sordid and cheap. If she could just get John away from the store for a while... impossible. With Lina still in care, John is pulled in every direction. Rosemarie will just have to be patient.

When Rosemarie finally gets home from work on Friday, she sees the mail laying on the counter. She peruses it while she plugs the kettle in to make tea. Among the bills and the usual junk mail Rosemarie sees an envelope from MD labs that's been ripped open. It's not addressed to anyone, nor does it bear a postmark and Rosemarie is tempted to look inside when she hears Frankie yell at her from upstairs. "Call your sister, Rose!"

Rosemarie finds Frankie poring over some documents and

asks him what he's up to. Frankie tells Rosemarie that he's filling in forms from Master Locks Academy of Hair Design.

"Oh, yeah. How did you do on your test?"

"Fine, I got the results back today. Don't worry I'm HIV negative."

"What are you talking about, Frankie?"

"My blood test. Did you think it was some kind of multiple choice quiz?" Frankie imitates a game show host. *True or False: Do blondes have more fun?*"

"Very funny. But why do you need to take blood tests for beauty school? Sorry, *hair design*." Frankie told Rosemarie she's not supposed to call it that anymore. Nor is she to refer to a stylist as a "hairdresser."

"Duh. Hep B, scissors, blood. Hello? If I cut myself *and* the client, we might as well have swapped gob. Anyhow, don't get too excited. Between tuition, books and supplies, it costs more than $10,000 to enroll in their one-year course. The next session starts in the spring and a friend of mine who works there offered to let me sit in on some classes to see if I'd like it. He insists that I meet the entrance requirements or I won't be able to participate."

"Oh." Rosemarie feels so foolish. "I had no idea it was so expensive."

"Yeah, well, besides not having the ten large, I can't leave the store at a time like this. My family needs me."

"I understand, and don't worry, Frankie. Your secret is safe with me." Rosemarie steers the conversation away from Frankie's family and back to safety. "What did my sister want?"

"She wants to show you the costume. She says it's just about done and ready for a fitting."

Roseanna is out, so Rosemarie leaves her a voice mail. She tells her that she'll stop by sometime over the weekend if she gets a chance. Rosemarie explains that between preparing for an audit and her job interview next week, she's wiped out. Rosemarie calls back again on Saturday only to be told that between chauffeuring the girls around town and becoming an internationally acclaimed costume designer, Roseanna's a bit busy.

Rosemarie manages to pop in to see her mother on Sunday afternoon for a short visit. When her mom complains that she never sees Rosemarie and wants to know what's been going on in her life, Rosemarie makes an excuse and leaves. She doesn't want to fill her mother in on the shenanigans at home or at work.

Lina's Incarceration

Gord finds Lina in the common room staring out the window. She is relieved to see Gord, especially since he's brought her the *Globe and Mail*. While they stroll back to Lina's room, they talk in hushed voices. "Thank, God," Lina says. "There's nothing to read here but the Bible, self-help brochures, and a dog-eared copy of *One Flew Over the Cuckoo's Nest*."

"How are ya, Lina? I mean *really?*"

"Hanging in, Gord. Hanging in."

Gord tells Lina he got rid of the "junk," and Lina says she's got some more for him. "Can't you just flush them down the toilet?" Gord asks.

"Are you kidding?" Lina lowers her voice when she remembers their covert operation requires secrecy. "They don't let you go by yourself. And those things won't go down these low-flush jobs they got in here. Not enough pressure."

"Yeah, well you're really putting the pressure on me."

"I know, Gordo, and I'm sorry for that, but there's no one else I can trust. Here," she whispers. Lina hands Gord another wad of Kleenex.

Gord pockets it without further objection. "I can't believe you're getting away with this," Gord says. When he asks Lina how she does it, Lina tells Gord some yarn about it being an old circus trick and she claims to have a "double-jointed tongue."

"There's not as many here as last time," Gord says. "Did you have to take some?"

"No, they're weaning me off the smack. This social interaction of ours has them believing it's the reason I'm improving."

"Can you at least tell me why you're in here?"

"You're strictly on 'need to know,' Gordo. Consider it a little vacation on the funny farm."

"Roger, that. Can I bring you anything else to read?" Gord asks. "Conrad Black's new book is out. There's an article in the paper about him tearing a strip out of some dude from the BBC. It says your man threatened to punch him in the face. Black still claims he's not a criminal."

"He was set up," Lina declares. Conrad Black is Lina's hero. "Better bring a dictionary too," she adds. "That way I can work on my vocabulary while I'm looking for tips. Without it, I won't have a clue what he's talking about."

"Tips?"

"How to cope while I'm on the inside," Lina confides with a wink.

Gord fills Lina in as best he can on the goings-on at the store. He answers Lina's questions about the new bookkeeper. "She's a looker," Gord tells Lina. "She's got all the fellas in a dither. Your boys included, especially John. You know Frankie moved in with her?"

"I heard. What do you mean, 'especially John?' My Johnny's a good boy."

"Hey, don't get me wrong. John's got good taste. Rose is very nice and she's helping out a lot. You should be happy," Gord scolds Lina. "Poor kid has to cover for you, and now I hear she's got the tax man breathing down her neck to boot. It's very stressful for her, you know. And FYI, Frankie's just her roommate. Rose was going to lose her fabulous pad, so Frankie is helping her out, too. He can't stop talking about it, says it's a palace–on *Superior Street* if you can believe it. And Nick doesn't seem to mind. With him working evenings and Frankie on days, he says it don't make much difference to him."

"God, I miss my boys."

"I know, Lina. Get your shit together, whatever it is you're up to. That's what you're always telling me, eh?"

"That's right. And don't worry! I got a plan and I'm on schedule."

Gord doesn't stay long. They run a tight ship and it's nearly supper time. When he leaves, Lina scans the *Globe* looking for the latest scoop on Lord Black of Cross Harbour.

XVI

Christine Constantine arrives early Tuesday morning to begin her audit and waits for Rosemarie in Lina's office. At Christine's behest, Rosemarie spends the day looking up various documents. "It's a pretty straightforward routine," Christine says. "It shouldn't take more than a day or two."

Christine and Rosemarie spend the next two days going about their respective tasks. Christine isn't fazed by Lina's books, in fact she tells Rosemarie she's seen a lot worse. Christine says a lot of small business owners shove all their receipts and bills haphazardly into a shoe box and expect their accountant to muddle through it.

On Thursday morning, when John pops into the office to check on them, Rosemarie lets him know that she will have to leave early to attend a job interview. He looks concerned, but doesn't object.

"You're lucky," Christine tells Rosemarie. "Not every woman has a boss that nice. And he's not hard to look at either," Christine remarks. The comment takes Rosemarie by surprise. It's not that she disagrees with Christine's assessment, it's just that it's out of character for Christine. Over the last two days, Rosemarie and Christine had many opportunities to talk, but they kept the conversation focussed on financial matters and accounting. That's the sort of effect John has on women, Rosemarie notes. Even women who are all business can't help themselves. For a moment Rosemarie feels proud, then in turn, silly, so she doesn't respond. When Christine asks to take a closer look at some of the deposit slips, Rosemarie is relieved to be able to excuse herself. Should any tricky questions arise, she doesn't want to be tempted to lie on Lina's behalf. Rosemarie hurries home to change.

Rosemarie imagines stepping into her walk-in closet is like stepping into the ladies' cloakroom at the United Nations, if such a place exists. The back wall displays an impressive array of footwear from around the globe. Each pair is tucked into its own cubbyhole and arranged floor-to-ceiling in ascending order of stature. Her eyes flash up to the top and land in Spain, where Manolo kitten heels nuzzle up to her favourite Italians, the Bruno Magli red leather stilettos with patent-leather toes. The seam between the shiny and matte kid skin is sealed with a delicate gold chain that wraps across the top of the arch. Rosemarie plucks them from their nest and gives them an affectionate smooch before choosing their shorter Italian cousins one level below: black leather pumps favoured by Alitalia air hostesses for their practical style and comfort. They'll make a perfect match for the charcoal grey suit Rosemarie has decided to wear.

Another pair of black pumps sit beside the Magli's. Although not nearly as practical, these babies are hand-crafted in peau de soie by Stewart Weitzman, who insists shoes should be sexy *and* comfortable. As if he's been reading Rosemarie's mind, Mr.

Weitzman says, "A girl wants her shoe to enter the room before her, and she wants it to be there after she leaves."

The middle zone holds those great Danes: Remonte Dorndorfs in aniline leather dyed the colour of the North Sea; Dortmüend ballet flats; and Ecco sandals that feel like she's walking on a cloud. Another pair of sandals, these ones made in Hungary by Josef Seibel, are the exact colour of Lake Superior on a stormy day and feature cleverly disguised magnetic and velcro closures.

The sensible shoes are closer to the ground where the down-to-earth Birkenstocks mingle with the Romikas, while Doc Marten holds court.

Rosemarie's meat slippers live at the store.

One space of honour is reserved at the top for the Jimmy Choo sling backs Rosemarie was planning on buying the next time she went to the "Big Smoke." That plan went up in smoke with her unexpected trip to the unemployment office. Now Rosemarie can't foresee getting to Toronto before they're out of style. Should she dare to expect to own them in this lifetime? A girl can dream.

The first dusting of snow melted without the aid of salt, so Rosemarie prances confidently down the street without worrying about ruining her shoes or having to wear boots and change when she gets there. Rosemarie turns north on Cumberland Street toward the Prince Albert Hotel, where the Golden Daffodil team from Toronto are conducting interviews for middle-management positions.

Rosemarie presumes the head-hunters are in a big hurry to wrap things up and fly back to Toronto. When they called with a request to reschedule her interview, Rosemarie was told that they were making good progress and hoped to accomplish their goals in less time than they had originally anticipated. She accepted the new time-slot on short notice, knowing that it would be suicidal to say no. Rosemarie would never have accepted a "no" when she was the one conducting interviews and made such a request. If an applicant seriously wants the job, they'll go to hell and back to conform to the whims of the interviewer, even if it means shirking their present responsibilities. Strange, that. It's ironic because one of the things Rosemarie always studied when considering a prospective employee is how they treated their present or past employers.

Rosemarie sometimes took a peek at an applicant's Facebook page to see if they had bad-mouthed their boss. She used a phony profile, set up specifically to aid her clandestine snooping. Rosemarie didn't make it a habit, she only resorted to this nefarious digging if she suspected the applicant was projecting a far different image than the one Rosemarie saw seated across from her. If she was right, Rosemarie could prevent a disaster by not hiring the person. Rosemarie is big on prevention after her experience with that band of misfits at the McTavish. It's easier to weed them out before they require pruning; that's Rosemarie's creed.

Rosemarie caught more than one poser by using this method. Some people are such dopes when it comes to social networking. It's shocking to see the sort of personal information someone will reveal to the world without a second thought. A guy who claims his hobbies include any number of daring activities, often turns out to be a fake, and his only daring activity is posting lies on his blog, with photos to prove it hung on his "virtual" wall.

As she nears the hotel, Rosemarie's confidence begins to wane. She frets over her outfit. She worries about what the

Torontonians will think. Rosemarie has been so wrapped up in raw meat that she hasn't even seen this year's fall fashion collections. What will the people from "The Centre of the Universe" think of last year's suit? They'll know she's down and out. Or worse, they'll think she's a hick from the bush.

Rosemarie arrives with a couple of minutes to spare. She scurries off to the ladies' room to check her image in the mirror. She looks haggard. No amount of concealer can cover the dark lines that encircle her eyes. Her skin looks pasty and ashen in spite of a layer of foundation and a generous dusting of blush. Too much time underground, Rosemarie speculates. She applies a fresh coat of pink lipstick and musses up her hair, then combs it back into a more business-like attitude. Rosemarie takes a moment for positive affirmation. She looks at her reflection and repeats her mantra: "I am strong. I am confident. I am a winner." Her voice echoes off the tiled walls and floor. Rosemarie panics when she hears a toilet flush. *Oh, Christ! What if it's one of the Golden Daffodil people?*

Rosemarie tries to flee before she can be seen, but her hands are shaking and she drops her purse on the floor. She stops to collect the contents that have spilled out. Rosemarie is on her hands and knees when an elderly woman emerges from the stall. "I admire Helen Reddy, too," the blue-haired lady says. "The acoustics are great in here. Are you into that karioke thing, dear?"

Great. Now Rosemarie feels like a loser. She hobbles off to her interview trying to pull her skirt down to cover the tear in the knee of her stocking.

Rosemarie knows her résumé is airtight and impressive. The interview itself is remarkably brief, HR professional on HR professional being a tricky one, like well-matched combatants in the same weight class. Only it's three, against one. Two women and a token male who acts like he's in charge. They take turns grilling Rosemarie on policy and procedure.

Everything is going smoothly until they get to the question about short term vs long term goals. In Rosemarie's experience, there's only one correct answer: she sees herself sitting in their position on the other side of the desk. In the position of power. In effect saying that she isn't satisfied to be the understudy, she wants to be the star. So everyone, including Rosemarie herself, is shocked when they ask her where she sees herself in the next year, and Rosemarie answers, "I have no idea." That's definitely not the answer they are expecting. She's an HR professional for God's sake!

Following this revelation, the interview comes to a rather abrupt close. They give Rosemarie the usual line about being in touch soon. So quick are they to dismiss her, Rosemarie gets the impression they had made their decision before they had begun. Rosemarie doesn't dare to allow herself to believe it's *her* they'd chosen. Especially after she botched her answer about her goals. Rosemarie can barely recall what she said now that the interview is over. She prays it wasn't as lame as she thinks.

When Rosemarie gets back to the store, Christine is loading boxes of files into her car. Like déjà vu, Christine promises Rosemarie she'll be hearing from her soon.

That's it? It can't be that easy, Rosemarie thinks with a sigh of fatigue, more than relief. She takes the opportunity to go home and get some rest.

Rosemarie has the weekend off and spends most of it in bed. She is so burned out from the hectic week at work, stressed about the audit, anxious about the outcome of her interview, not to mention the fiasco with Lina and the cash, that she needs the rest. The whole thing is making her sick. Rosemarie is unsure about her feelings for John. One thing is certain: she can't get him off her mind. While she recuperates, Rosemarie continues to deliberate on the subject. The jury is still out when Monday morning rolls around.

True to her word, Christine concludes her forensic enquiries and returns Falcone's files early in the week. Christine tells Rosemarie she only found a couple of minor abnormalities on the books and she's willing to overlook them in light of the present situation.

Rosemarie had reminded Christine that she was filling in temporarily for Lina. She fleshed out the excuse by telling Christine in confidence that Mrs. Falcone is presently under a psychiatrist's care being treated for schizophrenia.

Christine is impressed that they are implementing a computerized accounting system. "Most of these family run businesses don't want to change," she tells Rosemarie. "And that's usually the kiss of death. When the next generation takes over, they can't believe how hard their parents worked. Either they can't maintain that work ethic, or they've become professionals—lawyers, engineers, accountants, you name it—and they don't have to do the sort of menial labour that put them through university in the first place." Christine admits that her own parents ran a Greek restaurant and finally retired when she got hired at CRA and they knew for certain that she would not be taking over the family business. Christine figures that's why a lot of the independent "greasy spoons" are disappearing. A lack of cheap labour, combined with their refusal to change, means they can't compete once the chains muscle in.

To Rosemarie's astonishment, Christine is convinced the irregularities are mistakes, especially after she discovered the unclaimed HST input tax credits. The error was only duplicated once, on the previous quarterly return, which effectively demonstrated, if not proved, that Lina had been competent until recently. "It's perfectly understandable given that Mrs. Falcone was functioning in a diminished capacity as a result of her mental health issues," Christine says.

Christine thanks Rosemarie for her cooperation while Rosemarie walks her out to her car. She wonders if Christine might want to conclude the audit before the government end up owing the Falcones any more money.

When Rosemarie tells John the good news, he is visibly relieved. When she shares further good news; that they will be allowed to deduct the unclaimed HST credits from future payments, John brightens up considerably.

"You're really something, Rose. I owe you."

"All in the line of duty, boss."

Rosemarie is pleased to be finished with this mess. She takes the opportunity to remind John that it will be easier to find a replacement for Lina now that the new software is up and running.

"I can help recruit someone," Rosemarie offers. "Even if I don't get the job I applied for." She wants to ease the blow. If Rosemarie doesn't get hired at the new hotel, she may have to consider moving out of town. This is not something she wants to do, but it may become necessary. Rosemarie sent résumés out to every place in town she can think of, yet she hasn't received a single call.

"I got a feeling Lina will be back to her old self soon," John says. "Maybe I won't have to replace her."

Sheesh! Doesn't he get it?"

"But will Lina be willing to learn a new accounting program? Rosemarie asks.

"She'll have to. It's a done deal. And like you said, I'm the boss," John brags.

Rosemarie wonders if John is joking. With what she knows about John's mother, it's likely that Lina will decide for herself if and when she wants to return to work.

"Maybe Lina will want to take this opportunity to retire," Rosemarie says.

"Maybe. Whatever happens," John says, "I still owe you. I'd like to take you out for a proper thank-you dinner this weekend. That is, if you're not busy. We should celebrate."

"Well, John," Rosemarie hesitates. "I don't really have any plans but it seems an odd thing to be celebrating."

"Great!" John says. How about Superior Bistro? The owner shops here all the time and he always needles me about never coming to his place."

Superior Bistro is the most expensive restaurant in town. All the mucky-mucks go there and rave about the food. How can Rosemarie say no to John? He's so relieved to be done with the audit, and he's still got his mother to worry about. Besides, he seems so excited. And Rosemarie could use a night out, too.

"Okay, John," Rosemarie says. "It's pretty expensive though, are you sure you don't want to go somewhere less fancy?"

"You're worth it, Rose. I'll make a reservation for Saturday night. Is eight o'clock okay?"

"Sure, John. That sounds great."

"Wear something pretty," John says. "We'll do it up right!"

When John found out about the audit, he questioned Gord a little further. John asked Gord what made him think Lina was not taking her medication. Gord dropped a handful of pills all lumped together in a wad of Kleenex onto John's desk and said, "exhibit A." Gord said he had no idea why she was doing it but he was convinced Lina was in her right mind, if not perfectly sane. Gord told John that he felt it was his duty to stand by Lina in her time of need, whatever the heck it was, and he admitted that he agreed to smuggle the drugs off the ward. Gord hung onto the pills in case he had to prove it. Naturally, Gord didn't want to show John unless he was asked to.

After the conclusion of the audit, Gord told John how much better he thought Lina was doing. "I thought maybe my visits were helping," Gord said. "When I told Lina the auditor didn't find any problems, she really perked up. Guess she was under a lot of stress."

Thus enlightened, John went to see Lina's doctor and asked him to release Lina into his care. The doctor agreed, stating that he's never seen such a remarkable recovery in such a short time span. "Obviously, weaning her off the medication before she developed a dependency was the right course of action," the doctor said, taking credit for the decision when it was John who had begged the doctor to wean Lina off the drugs.

Lina's Release

"Okay, Lina. The jig is up."

"John, is that you? Is that my Johnny?"

"Never mind that psychobabble," John says. "I know what you did and I know why. When I found out you didn't claim a tax credit, I couldn't believe it. The more I thought about it, the less sense it made. Until I found out about the audit. You knew they'd find that HST mistake, didn't you? You knew they would think you were incompetent. And you knew I would think you had gone mad."

"Hey, I had to throw them a bone."

"So they wouldn't find out about the cash sales?"

"What cash? What do you mean?" Lina asks. Nobody would know if the stuff she wrote off was stolen or rotten. Even an experienced auditor would have trouble following her trail.

"I know about the cash Lina. I found it. Me and Rose–"

"I shoulda known."

"Rosemarie Catanzaro has been filling in for you."

"I know who she is. So what does she want, this *puttana* of yours?"

"Don't you dare–" John hisses like someone's let the air out of his tires. He is careful to lower his voice so the staff won't hear them. "She doesn't want anything. She's my... friend. And you're lucky it was Rose who figured it out. We'd be in big trouble if that auditor did."

Lina is impressed that Rosemarie was able to follow her trail. She covered her tracks better than Pierre Poutine. Lina was worried about the government sending some crackerjack kid trying to make a name for himself. Or worse, one who doesn't know his ass from a teakettle. You never know what they're gonna find if they dig deep enough.

"Call me paranoid," Lina says, like it's a good thing. "But let me tell you something that's as sure as death and taxes. There is no such thing as a *random* audit!"

"The thing is, why would you steal from yourself?" John asks. "I don't get it."

"All those *paesanos* always paid with cash and never wanted a receipt 'cause they didn't want to pay taxes," Lina says. "And that was only PST. Long before the goddamned GST, never mind HST! Don't get me started. And if I wrote off the stock, it lowered our profits. For chrissake, Johnny, the government's got their nose so far up our *keesters*, between PST and GST... 'scuse me, now it's HST... not to mention payroll taxes! By the time we make any money they wanna grab another twenty five percent for corporate income tax. And if I paid you and the boys more, you'd be in a higher personal tax bracket. I did it for you!"

"And just what the heck were you going to do with all that cash?"

"I don't know, maybe send you boys to get a good education so you wouldn't have to work as hard as your father and your uncle did. And it wasn't that much, not in the beginning. It just kind of accumulated over the years."

"Well, I'm sorry to disappoint you."

"I'm not disappointed in you or your cousins. I'm proud. Always have been."

"Get your stuff, mom. We're blowing this pop stand."

XVIII

When Saturday evening arrives, Rosemarie still feels a little worn out and wonders if she's coming down with something. John seems far too excited for Rosemarie to back out of their date, and she's looking forward to it, too. She's been walking on Grade A shells all week. At least they'll have some privacy away from the store and the prying eyes and pricked ears of the staff. Finally, they'll be able to discuss what happened between them and maybe decide where to go from here.

Rosemarie takes great care choosing what to wear. Nothing too revealing, yet something soft and feminine; a complete departure from the attire John normally sees her in. The weather has turned cold enough to merit digging into her winter wardrobe. Rosemarie decides on a butter coloured lambs' wool sweater with a ballet neck and her Dress-Stuart tartan pencil-skirt with navy tights. This is Rosemarie's favourite outfit to wear as soon as the temperature drops below freezing. Smart casual. She ponders whether she should dare to

207

wear her red heels. She opts for low ankle boots instead. A girl doesn't wear *Come Fuck Me* shoes when she's trying to slow things down.

John said he'd pick Rosemarie up at quarter to eight. He's three minutes early and she's ready to go.

Rosemarie didn't tell Frankie she was going out with John tonight. Luckily Frankie is getting ready to go out with his new friends from hair design school. When the door intercom rings, Rosemarie calls out, "See you later, Frankie." To avoid what could be an awkward situation, Rosemarie runs down to greet John, instead of buzzing him in. From the parking lot Rosemarie sees Frankie at the window. Frankie waves at them and Rosemarie regrets she didn't sneak out.

Superior Bistro is packed. Every table is occupied and in spite of being on time for their reservation, the maitre d' tells John it will be about ten minutes before he can seat them. He apologizes profusely, and suggests they wait at the bar.

John looks fabulous. He's wearing brushed cotton chinos and an open neck linen shirt under a soft black leather jacket. His white shirt is ironed so perfectly, Rosemarie wonders if he did it himself. When she starts to wonder whether he looks better with or without the shirt, she forces her mind back into the present. Not one hair on his head is out of place. That seems like a safe opener, so she asks John if Frankie cuts it.

"Yeah, he always cuts my hair. Nick's, too."

"He really is very good, isn't he? It looks nice, John."

"You look great, Rose. It's so nice to see you without your uniform on. I mean, dressed up," John says, correcting his faux pas.

While John acts like an awkward teenager, Rosemarie spots a group of familiar-looking people seated around a table for eight. When she realises who they are, Rosemarie turns her back to them before she is seen.

As Rosemarie turns away to face the bar, John says, "I'm sorry, that sounded like a cheesy pick-up line."

"What? Oh, forget it. I knew what you meant." Rosemarie dismisses John's apology with a wave. "I just recognized some of the board members sitting over there. That's my old boss at the far end of that table. He's the one making all the fuss.

John spins around and cranes his neck to see who Rosemarie is talking about. A group of guys in suits are laughing at a bald guy who's telling a joke.

Rosemarie is suddenly very uncomfortable. She wants to leave and isn't sure if John will be offended. "To tell you the truth, John, I'm not that hungry. And this place is so busy, I'm sure they won't mind if we leave." *Not to mention, expensive* she thinks, *and noisy, too.* They have to shout to be heard and no one has taken their order for drinks yet. "I don't feel like a big meal. If it's alright with you, we could go to this Lebanese place that serves great salads and kebabs. It's at the other end of town and it's a little more laid back."

"In *Fort William?*"

"Yeah, is that okay?"

"Sure, Rose, anything you want." John agrees without further hesitation. "I'll tell the waiter."

Not more than fifteen minutes later Rosemarie and John are seated together in a booth in a small restaurant with only a few tables occupied; a group of four people talk quietly while an elderly man chats with the waiter. A young couple study the menu and don't say a word to each other.

The waiter brings Rosemarie and John a couple of menus and John asks to see the wine list.

"Oh, I forgot. This place doesn't have a liquor license," Rosemarie tells John. She shrugs at the Arab waiter. "I used to come here for lunch when I worked over at the board. I've never been here in the evening."

"That's okay with me," John says. "But we can go somewhere else if you want."

"I'm fine with water," Rosemarie says. The waiter offers them the option to order take-away.

"No, we're good. Thanks, buddy. Water's fine with me, too." Apparently John doesn't mind a teetotalling date.

They start with *Labneh;* strained yoghurt drizzled with olive oil and topped with chopped mint leaves. It's served with pita triangles to scoop up the creamy dip and it's meant to be shared. Rosemarie orders *fattoush;* a tossed salad similar to what every Greek restaurant in town serves, minus the olives and feta. Instead, it's garnished with fried strips of pita and smothered in a tangy lemon vinaigrette. It's Rosemarie's favourite item on the menu. John orders a beef kebab and *fattoush,* taking Rosemarie's advice to save room for dessert. "They have a wonderful selection of pastries made with filo and stuffed with custard cream or pistachios and honey. It's similar to baklava but better," Rosemarie tells John.

"This is delicious," John says between mouthfuls. "I had no idea this place existed."

"I know. I love it. I guess this is behind enemy lines for you."

The way John pronounced *Fort William,* like it was a foreign country, reminds Rosemarie that John's parents fell into the "diehard" category. John always calls the north side of Thunder Bay, *Port Arthur.* "I hope you didn't mind driving all the way over here. At least you didn't have to go home to get your passport."

"I still get lost over here," John admits.

"Just head for the lake and you'll be fine."

"This is nice," John says.

Rosemarie isn't entirely sure if John means the food or their date. "Yeah. We kind of got off... " Rosemarie struggles to find the right words for what happened. "... on the wrong foot."

"I agree."

At last, they're going to talk about what matters. "You must think I'm some kind of... "

"I think you're great, Rosie."

"Well, I want you to know that what happened... " Again, Rosemarie is too embarrassed to put it into words. "... at the office–"

"Should stay at the office," John says, finishing Rosemarie's sentence.

"It's just that things are moving so quickly. Maybe we should start fresh."

"So I guess my marriage proposal is out of the question then?" John says.

They both laugh at John's silliness.

"Not 'til you buy me a rock and get down on one knee, Falcone. But seriously, John, I'd like to see you again. Socially I mean, but it's very awkward. I think we should take things a lot slower."

"Okay," John says. "It'll give me time to save up."

"For what?"

"That ring."

They spend the rest of the evening in the comfort of their shared childhood, chatting about school and comparing what they know about half-forgotten classmates. It's a relief for Rosemarie to be away from the hubbub of headquarters. They linger over dessert, although Rosemarie asks the waiter to wrap hers to take home. She orders mint tea, glad that there was no wine to add confusion to her already confused head. John orders Lebanese coffee, a stronger sweeter version of Turkish coffee. When he takes the first sip, John says he'll be up all night. Inevitably, the conversation turns towards work.

John tells Rosemarie that Lina has been released and is at home doing well. "Once she's up to it, she'd like to meet 'the woman who saved her ass,'" John says. "That's how Lina put it," he explains. "She wants to thank you for your help while she was *indisposed*. Her word for it, not mine," John says.

"What about the money?"

"For now, it's in the safe. Lina claims she always meant to use it for our education, but me and the twins never went to university, so she didn't know what to do with it. She said hardly anyone uses cash nowadays, so it doesn't come up that often anymore. She promised she won't do it again."

"You mean she's coming back to work?" Rosemarie asks.

"She'd like to. I told her I'd have to think it over. She was faking, you know. To get out of the audit, or to cover her butt if she got caught, I presume. I told her I'd have to think about it because we've made some significant changes while she was fooling around."

"Your mom knows about the new accounting system?"

"Yeah. She says she'll give it try, but I don't know... I'd rather she retired. She's worked hard her whole life and she's not getting any younger."

"You're a good son, John. Lina is very lucky."

John leans across the table and looks like he's going to kiss Rosemarie. Instead he covers her hand with his. "Thank you, Rose. For everything."

Rosemarie smiles and stifles a yawn. "It's late, we should go."

John finds his way back to Rosemarie's place without the aid of GPS. They sit for a minute while the engine idles. Before John can make a move, Rosemarie leans over and kisses him gently on the lips.

"You're welcome," she says. Rosemarie notices that John waits until she's safely inside her building before he drives away.

XIX

Now that she's no longer working in the meat department, Rosemarie has weekends off. She welcomes her old habit of languishing in bed on Sunday mornings, although she has to get up to pee again. In spite of not drinking anything last night, Rosemarie feels a bit hungover. Her mind wanders back to her date with John while her hands wander around her own naked body, touching herself with intense pleasure at the mere thought of him. She rolls over and recalls a vision of John in his crisp linen shirt leaning in to kiss her. Did he change his mind because he's too shy for a public display of affection? or out of respect for her wish to slow things down? Mmm, Rosemarie's hands travel up to cup her breasts which are swollen and tender. It occurs to Rosemarie that she should have had her period by now. *Stress can do that*, she thinks. And she's been under a lot of it lately.

Hopefully, the pressure's off. Seeing those men from the board of education last night made Rosemarie appreciate her new life. All this time she's been feeling sorry for herself, and now Rosemarie is almost glad she lost her job at the board. She's glad to be quit of them, that's for sure. And if it wasn't for that fiasco, Rosemarie would never have rekindled her... what? Friendship? Rosemarie doesn't know what to call her relationship with John.

Rosemarie was starting to seriously consider taking over Falcone's bookkeeping full-time, even though she wouldn't make nearly as much money. Now, Lina's remarkable recovery threatens that option. Prestige, not only money, had motivated Rosemarie to want the HR position. Being in a position of power and hanging out with the well-heeled crowd used to be what she wanted. Now Rosemarie doesn't know what she wants for breakfast, let alone her future. Coffee, and maybe some dry toast, that's what she wants for breakfast. John? Is that what she wants for her future?

"Morning, Rose," Frankie says from behind the newspaper. He sits at the dining room table drinking a cup of coffee. "Have a good time last night?"

Rosemarie doesn't know what to tell Frankie. She grabs a mug and pours herself some coffee. Frankie saw her go out with John so she can't lie to him. "Yeah. You?"

"Yeah, it was great. I met a few students from the academy at Bar Italia and we had some laughs. How was Superior Bistro?"

Rosemarie keeps her tone casual. "Actually, we went somewhere else. You knew I had a date with John?"

Frankie peeks over the top of the paper and gives her an odd inquisitive look. "Who do you suppose ironed his shirt?"

Jesus Christ-in-a-linen-shirt! What doesn't he know?

"What have you got planned today?" Frankie asks.

That's odd. Isn't he going to push me for details? "Oh, not much. Thought I'd better go see my sister before she sends out the search and rescue."

Rosemarie drops a couple slices of bread into the toaster and Frankie drops the subject. He slurps up the dregs of his coffee and rinses his cup. "Say hi to Roseanna for me. I gotta get going or I'll be late for work. See you later, doll."

After Frankie leaves, Rosemarie takes a long bath. Again, she lets her mind drift toward John, this time she focusses on his gorgeous physique. The way his pants fit just so, the way his shirt strains against his broad shoulders, the way he looks at her. How could she have been so blind? She's known John forever, yet she's seeing him in a completely different light. That thought triggers another, as Rosemarie recalls their bodies lit up by florescent lights. Candlelight, she decides, would be better. Everyone looks better in the dark. Except John, that is. A clear vision of John shines brightly in Rosemarie's head.

Rosemarie phones her sister. Roseanna says she has no plans so Rosemarie tells her she'll walk over for a visit. She pulls on her old jeans and struggles to do them up. A few weeks behind a desk and she feels the weight of it. *Too much salami and not enough physical labour*, Rosemarie tells herself. A walk will do her good. Doing without a car has its advantages, but Rosemarie needs to make sure she's dressed for the weather.

Upstairs, Rosemarie checks the thermometer on the deck which announces the onset of winter with a severe drop in temperature, typical for Thunder Bay in late November. She looks out at the lake and sees only a few freighters bobbing at anchor in the harbour. Most of the lakers sailed before the big freeze. They won't be back until the ice breaker clears a path to re-open the shipping lanes in March. Back downstairs, she rummages through the bottom drawer of her dresser and looks for a scarf and a pair of mitts to keep her warm.

Rosemarie steps out into the bright sunlight and inhales clean clear air until her nostrils stick together. She wraps her scarf a little tighter and heads up Superior Street. Rosemarie passes some children drawing on the sidewalk with a piece of chalk. "A bit cold for hopscotch, isn't it?" Rosemarie says.

The kid with the chalk says, "We're playing Crime Scene." One of the kids is lying on the sidewalk with her limbs askew while another chalks an outline around the *"victim's"* body.

Rosemarie does a double-take. A splattered trail of red paint leads to another chalk outline further down the street.

"Where'd you get the chalk?" Rosemarie asks the kids.

"Cops left it behind," the one lying prone says.

Rosemarie takes a closer look around and sees a baseball bat with its red paint peeling off. With growing horror, she realises that the bat isn't painted red. It's blood. "Where'd you get the bat?"

"Found it behind that shed," the *"coroner"* says. "Don't touch it," she tells Rosemarie. "It's evidence."

Roseanna is already cooking up a feast. When Rosemarie steps into her sister's kitchen the smell of fried fish hits her. "Whoa, Mare, you look like the walking dead," Roseanna remarks.

Once she removes her mitts, coat, hat, and scarf, Rosemarie bends over to undo her boots. She feels faint. Now she's sweating. "I feel a little dizzy," Rosemarie tells her sister. "Can I have a glass of cold water?"

Roseanna draws a glass of water straight from the tap. The water coming out of Lake Superior at this time of year doesn't need ice. "Billie came in sixth overall at Sectionals."

Rosemarie is ashamed to admit she forgot all about that. She didn't even make it around to look at the costume Roseanna made. She drinks her water and doesn't respond.

"Anyhow, she doesn't turn fourteen till next August, so she still has another shot at Juvy next year," Roseanna says.

"She must be disappointed." Rosemarie is aware of how competitive Billie is.

"Not really. If you can believe it, she blamed it on the costume! Said I made the skirt too long. I told her there's no way any daughter of mine is going to parade around like a slut."

The impact of that comment shows in Rosemarie's expression. Roseanna eyes Rosemarie and continues, "Of course I didn't say it like that. What's wrong, you tie one on last night?"

"I didn't have anything to drink. I had a date."

"Muslim or recovering alcoholic?"

"With John," Rosemarie says. Refreshed from the water and her walk, Rosemarie feels less decomposed.

"John Falcone?" Roseanna blurts out. "Spill. I want details."

"Nothing happened. We went for dinner."

Roseanna waits for more. Rosemarie gives in, "Okay, not last night."

"But it happened?"

"Did it ever."

"So why do you look like your dog died?"

"Just tired, I guess. I've been under a lot of stress."

Again, Roseanna waits for details that are not forthcoming. Rosemarie cracks under her sister's gaze and says, "I accidentally fucked Frankie."

"What? You did what?"

"Well, you know, we were drunk... well, I was. And he was there... and I was... "

"Horny?"

"Yeah."

"Well I hope you used protection. I've just read the riot act to the girls. I've been reading this book, *How to Talk to Your Teenager About Sex*. I even used a banana to demonstrate the proper use of a condom. Would you believe they all just looked at me and said, 'we know, Mom,' as if I was an ancient relic holding a precious artifact."

Rosemarie loses whatever little colour she had. She feels like she might faint.

"Well, did you? Use protection?"

"Yes. No. I mean, I don't know. I remember asking him to, but the rest is kind of fuzzy. I can't remember what happened after that."

"When was this?"

"Three or four weeks ago."

"When was your last period?"

"I don't know."

"Jesus, Mare. You're like clockwork. Come on."

"Okay, I'm a week late. It's no big deal, Zanna, it's not morning sickness. I told you I've been under a lot of stress. I've been very busy."

"Yeah? Busy two-timing two cousins? First you tell me you

got a date with that dreamboat, John. Then you tell me you accidentally fucked his cousin. Yeah. I'd say you're under stress." Roseanna stands with her hands on her hips. This definitely wasn't covered in *How to Talk to Your Teenager*. "And by the way, what does that mean exactly? How do you accidentally fuck somebody?"

"I told you I was drunk... and horny! You can blame Timo for that. Besides, I thought Frankie was gay. One thing just led to another and... "

"Timo! What's that crazy butcher got to do with it?"

"I was dancing with him," Rosemarie says. "At a wedding at the *Itai*. It's his fault. He made me drink these horrible shots of sambuca and then he wouldn't take me home."

No further elaboration is required. Her sister is familiar with Rosemarie's inability to hold her liquor.

Rosemarie screws up her nerve and continues. "There's more, actually. John and I... "

"Tell me you didn't accidentally fuck him, too!"

"That one I did on purpose."

"Tell me you used protection!" Roseanna shouts. Rosemarie just shakes her head in response. Billie comes into the kitchen to see what all the fuss is about.

"Hey, Aunty Rose," Billie says. "What's up?"

Roseanna turns to face her youngest daughter. "Billie, tell Aunt Rose why you should never have sex without a condom."

"It's irresponsible?" Billie ventures.

"Correct," Roseanna says, turning back to face Rosemarie.

"You could get an STD?" Billie adds, like it's a pop quiz and she's on a roll.

"Good thing I trust my partner," Rosemarie says. *Make that, partners.*

Roseanna's eyes grow wild and she shakes her head "no," indicating to Rosemarie that it was the wrong thing to say.

"I mean, you're right, Billie," Rosemarie corrects herself. "It was irresponsible."

"Oh, my God," Billie gushes. "You mean this isn't a test? We're talking about *you*?"

"I'm afraid so, Billie."

"Are you preggers?" Billie asks, morphing back into the schoolgirl that she is.

"I don't know. Maybe."

"What are you gonna do?" Billie asks.

"I don't know."

Something very exciting occurs to Billie. "We're gonna get a cousin! Please, can we have a boy? *Pleeeze!*" she begs, like it's something you order off a menu. "There's too many girls in this family."

Billie's next-in-line sister, Bobbie hears the commotion and comes into the kitchen. Bobbie asks, "Who's knocked-up?"

Tears well up in Rosemarie's eyes. Roseanna sees the weight settle on Rosemarie's shoulders and takes control. "All right, that's enough. Leave us alone, girls. We have to talk."

"Aw, c'mon, Mom," Billie whines. "As soon as it gets good, I always get the boot."

"Yeah. It's not fair," Bobbie complains.

"Neither is life. Get over it," Roseanna says. She steers her daughters away from the kitchen and the topic. She looks at

Rosemarie as tears start to flow. "Motherhood. You ready for *that?*"

A box of Kleenex and an hour later, Roseanna says, "So, to recap, within three days you had sex with two out of three Falcones... what's wrong with Nick, by the way? Couldn't squeeze him in? One of which may or may not be gay, the other definitely a hunk of burnin' love, and now you may or may not be pregnant."

"That pretty much sums it up."

"And you may or may not be infected with God knows what," Roseanna frowns. "Especially when you tell me Frankie is... " Roseanna pauses, "... unisex."

"Well, if it's any consolation, I do know that Frankie doesn't have AIDS."

"How do you know? Did you ask him? Of course he'd say that!"

"He got tested and I saw the results. Admission requirements for hair design school," Rosemarie assures her sister before Roseanna's vivid imagination comes up with some other reason.

"C'mon, get your coat. Let's go," Roseanna orders.

"Where are we going?"

"The drugstore. We can start with a home pregnancy test and tomorrow you will march right down to the lab and get your blood tested."

Another hour later, from behind the closed bathroom door, Rosemarie can barely hear her sister's whispered questions. "I said, *Is it pink?* If the tip turns pink, you're doing it right."

"It's pink."

Silence while they wait for the results. Three minutes takes an eternity. At last, the kitchen timer rings. "Well?"

Rosemarie doesn't trust the test. It seems too simple. "I don't know. Maybe we should wait a little longer," she suggests.

"Is it positive or negative?"

"Plus sign," Rosemarie sniffs. She opens the door and hands the digital gizmo to her big sister. She says "Maybe it's a false-positive."

While they waited, Roseanna studied the information that came with the test. "Well, you're not on fertility drugs and you're not menopausal, so I don't think so. It says here, that a false-negative is pretty common. Especially if you take the test too soon."

Rosemarie had hoped for a different result. She says, "Maybe we should try the other test; the one with the lines."

"No way. These tests have come a long way since I had a bun in the oven. They're foolproof if you follow the instructions. Face it, little sister, I'm gonna be an aunt."

Rosemarie doesn't know whether to laugh or cry. She's done enough of the latter, and if she was going to do anymore, they'd have to go back to the drugstore to buy some more Kleenex. While they stood in line to buy the home-pregnancy test, Roseanna regaled Rosemarie with stories of her maternities. To hear Roseanna tell it, she got pregnant every time Eddie came to town. As the line-up eased toward the cash register, Roseanna had said, "I'm telling you the Catanzaro women are very fertile. Good thing Eddie works so far away, or I'd have a fuckin' soccer team by now." The cashier's dirty look matched Rosemarie's.

Rosemarie defers to her big sister's expertise. "Now what?" she asks.

"You get your pregnant ass over to the lab tomorrow."

Rosemarie feels queasy. She can no longer put it down to stress, although she's got a hell of a lot more of it now that she's confronted with pregnancy and the very real possibility of an infectious disease.

Early Monday morning, Rosemarie calls her doctor's office to make an appointment. Their office hours start early and end late, which was a compelling reason to switch to a private practice. It's a relief to no longer be forced to sit in the germ-infested waiting room of the Port Arthur Clinic.

The last time Rosemarie had an appointment there, she swore it would be her last. Rosemarie sat for ages straining to hear her name called out over the din of screaming snot-nosed brats running around like wild animals. While unmindful mothers flipped through ragged magazines and ignored them, oblivious to the micro bacteria that lurks between the pages they turned with licked fingers, the little monkeys climbed over everything, people included. Not one of them seemed concerned about the germs their kids were spreading. Rosemarie learned long ago to bring her own reading material and to never touch anything. If she wasn't sick when she arrived, she was by the time she left. Rosemarie missed her name when it was called and sat for almost an hour before she realised that she couldn't make out anything coming through the intercom over the clamour of the crowd. When Rosemarie went to remind the receptionist that she was still waiting, she was told that her name had been called three times before they bypassed her and called the next patient. When they finally called her again forty minutes later, Rosemarie's surname was mispronounced to the point where she almost didn't recognize it as her own.

So Rosemarie is delighted to get through to her new doctor's receptionist immediately. Rosemarie's delight evaporates when the receptionist tells her with the practised hostility essential for dealing with impatient patients, that unless it's a short consultation Rosemarie wishes to book, the next available appointment is not until the week after next. "In my experience," the receptionist tells Rosemarie, "everyone thinks their need is urgent, from a sore throat to a wart." When Rosemarie divulges the purpose of her visit, the receptionist defrosts. She tells Rosemarie she can squeeze her in later this week. She advises Rosemarie to contact the Thunder Bay District Health Unit in the meantime, should she want confidential rapid testing for STDs and infectious diseases.

Rosemarie's next call is to the Thunder Bay District Health Unit to find out if she needs an appointment. Press one for this, press two for that, *fuck it*. Rosemarie hangs up and gets ready for work. She'll try again later to see if she can get a human on the line.

By the time Rosemarie gets to work she's in a foul mood. John, on the other hand, is downright upbeat. He flashes her a smile bright enough to compete with a strobe light in a disco. "Good morning, sunshine," John says. You look... radiant today."

Oh, boy. Charming, too. Rosemarie screws on a low-wattage smile and says, "Morning, John," which is the best she can do. John walks with Rosemarie downstairs and waits while she stops in the staff room to grab a cup of coffee. "I thought I might show you how this program works later," Rosemarie says. "Maybe after lunch if you have some time."

"Actually, I wonder if you might show Lina. She's upstairs talking to the cashiers. She'll be down in a minute."

Just what she needs. Rosemarie had hoped for a quiet morning in the solitude of the office. Now she'll have to teach John's crazy mother how to turn on a computer. "Do you think she's up for that?" Rosemarie asks, with all the diplomacy she can muster.

"All that, and more," John answers cheerfully. "I just want to tell you how much I enjoyed our date the other night, Rose. It was really nice. I hope we can do that again soon."

"Yeah, sure. I mean, maybe." Rosemarie is not ready for this.

"Everything okay, Rose? You seem kind of... out of sorts."

"I don't feel too good today, John. I'll be fine, really. Should I get started, or wait for your mom?"

Lina descends the front stairs. "Here I am," she says. "You must be Rose."

Rosemarie extends her hand and says, "Rosemarie."

Lina ignores Rosemarie's hand and hugs her. "I just want to say thanks for covering my ass, Rose. John's a lucky guy. He tells me you're a whiz with the computer."

"Well, Mrs. Falcone... "

"Call me Lina. Even my boys do!"

"Okay, Lina. I can show you the accounting software I installed, if you like. It's a fairly simple program. If you're interested, I can teach you how to use it," Rosemarie says with reluctance.

"Does it come with a tutorial?"

"Yeah, I think so." *Tutorial? Where'd she pick up the lingo?*

"Great. That won't be necessary then," Lina says. I'm sure I can muddle through it. You can run along back up to the meat department. I'll call you if I need any... *guidance.*"

Rosemarie glances at John, who just shrugs. "Oh. All right," she says. Dismissed and dejected, Rosemarie is not pleased with the prospect of spending the day surrounded by raw meat. "Call me if I can help," she offers, but Lina and John have disappeared into the office.

Carol is glad to have another set of hands to help with the lunch prep and reels off instructions to Rosemarie as if she's new. Rosemarie detects a note of condescension in Carol's voice and wonders if she isn't pleased about Rosemarie's most recent fall from grace. Again.

The morning chores seem more tedious than ever. Time ticks by slowly. When Carol returns from her smoke break, Rosemarie takes the opportunity to try to make a quick phone call to the health unit. Unfortunately, when Rosemarie peeks into the office, Lina is tapping away at the computer like an old pro.

The day drags on. When Rosemarie takes her lunch break, she can only manage to swallow a little dry bread with a few vegetables. Hold the mayo, hold the cheese. Again, she attempts to make a phone call, and again, Lina is in the office with her nose in the books. At last, Rosemarie sees Nick come in for his evening shift and she's able to go home.

Rosemarie is not surprised to find an envelope in her mailbox sporting the Golden Daffodil logo. She's been expecting a rejection letter from the hotel. Rosemarie is stunned when she picks up her voice mail and listens to a message from the Golden Daffodil's hiring team leader. It's an apology for not calling sooner. The hotel's representative explains that there was a communication breakdown. He said they sent out an information package before they reached Rosemarie to inform her that she is the successful candidate. Rosemarie listens to the message again and rips open the letter.

Dear Ms Catanzaro;

It is my pleasure to inform you that you have been chosen... The rest is mostly propaganda; the company's mission statement and goals, corporate structure, the usual bullshit.

She can't believe it. Thank God! Another thought gives birth to a sinking feeling that lands in the pit of Rosemarie's stomach.

Rosemarie hears Frankie come in and quickly shuffles the letter under a pile of bills. She asks Frankie how his day off was.

"Pretty good," Frankie says. He unloads a bag of groceries. "How was your day?"

"Terrible. Lina came back to work and I was sent back to the meat department. I wasn't feeling too well today."

"I heard Lina was home but I didn't know she was back at work already. Are you still on days, Monday to Friday?"

Oh, God. She hadn't thought of that! "I guess so, for now anyhow. Nobody said otherwise." She doesn't tell Frankie the news about landing her dream job. At the moment it's more of a nightmare. She's not sure what she's going to do yet. "Are you working tomorrow?" Rosemarie asks instead.

"Yeah," Frankie says. "Only one day off this week."

Rosemarie had thought of asking Frankie if she could borrow his car tomorrow, but decides against it. "I'm really tired, Frankie. I think I'll take a nap."

"Don't be long," Frankie says, brandishing a bottle of white wine. "I'm making mushroom risotto for supper!"

An hour later, Rosemarie ignores Frankie's call. She stays in her room and skips dinner. She doesn't want to face Frankie or the rich and creamy rice and fungus. Rosemarie hopes Frankie assumes she didn't hear him call and will leave her to sleep. When she hears Frankie clanking dishes into the dishwasher, Rosemarie gets up to phone her sister.

Roseanna jumps on her with so many questions, Rosemarie tunes out. When Roseanna finally shuts up, Rosemarie asks her to escort her to the lab the next day. Roseanna says she is glad to oblige, as long as Rosemarie doesn't mind making a few stops.

Next, Rosemarie calls the store. John answers. Rosemarie tells John she thinks she's coming down with something and won't be able to come to work tomorrow, possibly a few days. "By the way," Rosemarie says, "your mother seems to know her way around a computer pretty well."

"Yeah, isn't she something? She says she's got it all figured out. And here I thought Lina didn't know how it worked. Turns out, she didn't want me to know because she didn't want to have to use the computer for accounting. She even admitted that's how she knew how to fake being crazy. She says she Googled it. She's something else, my mom!"

Rosemarie promises to let John know when she's feeling well enough to return to work, and hangs up.

***

Roseanna takes Rosemarie to the health unit as promised and vets their many questions. She gives them hell for making it so difficult for people to get professional service with the dignity they deserve.

By the time Rosemarie emerges from her doctor's office late Wednesday, she knows she is pregnant and free of any STD's or infectious diseases. Only a baby to worry about now.

Rosemarie frets over her predicament. She is now faced with a difficult choice between motherhood and her career. She can't accept this prestigious position if she's pregnant. She'll be on maternity leave before the project gets under way, a cardinal sin in the world of glass ceilings. She can't afford not to work, especially if she's got a baby coming. And Rosemarie can't fathom how she can keep up her relentless schedule at Falcone, and bring up a child at the same time. Can't, can't, can't be done. Rosemarie's mind wanders back to her brief encounter with the women who live in subsidized housing up the street. She shudders. *Great. Full circle.* Rosemarie is worried about losing her apartment now, too.

Rosemarie has no intention of becoming an unwed mother on the dole. The only sensible solution she can come up with is to have an abortion.

.

Rosemarie manages to dodge two more calls from the Golden Daffodil's people. She can't keep hiding from them. She will have to make a decision. She calls John.

John assumes Rosemarie is calling to let him know she's ready to come back to work. He's wrong.

"We need to talk, John. Can you meet me for coffee this evening?" Rosemarie knows a quiet little place not more than a block away. She'd rather risk a private chat in public, than entertain John at home with Frankie around. Rosemarie stares out the blackened window and catches her reflection in the glass. She should take the time to fix herself up a little. Her eyes are red and puffy from all the crying and she looks like hell. Fortunately, Frankie assumes Rosemarie has a cold so he has steered clear of her for a few days, giving her time to think.

John tells Rosemarie he's making sausage and can't get away. Rosemarie asks if it's okay if she comes by to see him at the store. "Sure," John says, "I'm down in the dungeon. I'd love some company."

A half-hour later, Rosemarie finds John in the prep area. He's washing something in a hand basin and rinsing it under running water in the vegetable sink. John nods to a stool in the corner, inviting Rosemarie to sit down while he works. "What's up, Rose? You got a cold or something?"

"No," she says. "I've got some news, John."

John takes a closer look at Rosemarie. "Sorry I couldn't get away," he says.

Another reason that makes this an impossible situation. What kind of father would John be when he's constantly needed at work? The man does not know what it means to delegate.

"I want to make the sausage," Rosemarie declares, surprising both of them.

"Okay. Sure. Wash up first, and I'll show you how we do it," John says.

Rosemarie removes her jacket and sweater. She's wearing an old T-shirt and jeans. She scrubs up at the hand sink.

"You'll find a clean smock over there," John says, nodding at the hook by the door. "Better put that on and roll up the sleeves."

She follows John's instructions. Although the smock fits most of the guys snugly, it looks like it could fit Rosemarie in six or seven months. For now, she feels like a kid playing dress-up.

"I already ground and seasoned the pork," John says, "so now we're ready for the fun part. These are sheep gut." John removes a mile-long sausage casing from the sink and stuffs one end of the casing onto a tube sticking out of the grinder. "The sheep gut comes packed in salt to preserve it," he says. "We wash it until the water runs clear. Then we feed as much as we can onto the sausage stuffer, and tie it off like this."

Rosemarie had no idea that's how the meat got into its skin. It reminds her of the condom they should have used. *Too bad John didn't think of that!*

John indicates a plastic coated set of buttons. "Okay, Rose, fire it up," he says. "Green means go."

Rosemarie pushes the button and the huge contraption comes to life. Pink mush oozes into the translucent sheath. John holds the slowly filling end, while he skilfully guides it onto the stainless steel counter where he allows it to coil like a giant snake. "When the casing runs out, we twist this into links," he says. "You have to apply a bit of resistance and be careful to keep the thickness consistent without forming any air bubbles."

When John notices that he's nearly out of casing, he says, "Get ready to switch off the grinder, Rose. Okay... now." The end of the casing slips off while the grinder continues to churn out a bit of meat. With expert timing, John catches the ground pork in his hands and dumps it back into the hopper. John ties off the end and holds a length of coil between both hands. He gives it a little flip forward. A sausage forms and John repeats this magic trick, moving along the length of the coil until he's got a freshly linked chain. "Now we cut these apart and put them into a food bin. You can start that if you like while I thread more casings on. There's a clean bin over by the sink. If you see any air bubbles, give them a little prick with this." John hands Rosemarie a knife and what looks like a crochet hook, only sharper.

Rosemarie follows orders and starts to separate the links.

Of course she's seen the bins full of sausage arrive upstairs in the cooler marked with a piece of peach paper; "mild," "medium," and "hot." "Which ones are these?" Rosemarie asks, unable to judge which is which.

"These are mild," John says. "We usually start with mild, then add more chile pepper to the next batch. They get hotter as we progress." *Completely opposite to how we got started*, Rosemarie thinks.

John finishes threading the next length of casing and says, "Here, Rose. Why don't you try one?"

Rosemarie wraps her hand around the stuffing tube while John starts up the grinder. A giant ball of mush seeps out of the grinder but does not fill the casing the way it's supposed to. John shuts the motor off. "You have to ease up a bit," he tells Rosemarie. "Your grip is too tight." John cuts the end of the sheep gut, scoops the meat back into the hopper and ties it off once more. "Try again, Rose. You ready?"

"Ready as I'll ever be." This time the meat fills the casing as Rosemarie guides it onto the table. It's a little lumpy and looks more like a caterpillar than a snake. John slides his hands over the encased worm to smooth out the lumps. He tells Rosemarie to stop squeezing, reminding her to lighten up. It starts to resemble the one John made. Too quickly, the casing runs out while meat continues to seep out of the tube. The ground pork lands in the stainless steel bowl John placed in front of the grinder for this purpose. Rosemarie hits the red button and scoops the leftovers back into the hopper. "Wow. That was fun! Want me to thread the next length on?" Rosemarie asks.

"Sure, Rose. Look for a little red plastic tab in the basin; that's the starting end," John tells her. "You pull that off and start threading from that end until you can't fit any more on."

John fills a food bin with sausages and says, "I'll mark this and take it upstairs. I'll be right back. Don't start without me!"

"Okay, hurry up!" Rosemarie is so engrossed in the art of creation she nearly forgot what she came to discuss.

John is back by the time the casing is threaded and Rosemarie is ready to go. He starts up the beast and this time, Rosemarie fills and coils the length like a pro. "Looks like you don't need me," John says with a smirk and starts twisting it into links. "Wanna give this a try?"

"Yeah!"

John takes over the feeding, so Rosemarie is free to try her hand at linking. She picks up the coil, pinches the ends of what she thinks is about the right length and gives it a flip like John demonstrated. Rosemarie's sausage is a foot long. "That's okay," John says, "we can peel it when we cut them apart and add it back into the hopper."

"Sorry, John. I didn't know how long to make it." *I should have known... I've seen enough of them lately!*

"We try to make them about the size of the bun, but I like a little sticking out of both ends."

"Me too," Rosemarie agrees. "That way, your first bite is meat, not bread."

Nick brings down a stack of empty bins and looks surprised to see Rosemarie. "Hi, there, Rose." Nick inspects Rosemarie's gigantic sausage and grins.

"It's my first try," Rosemarie explains.

"Kind of phallic," Nicks says. "If we made them like that, all the girls would want one."

John gives Nick a look that says, *scram.*

"Just bringing you some clean bins," Nick says. "I better get back upstairs."

"Apparently, size does matter!" Rosemarie quips, not the least bit offended by Nick's judgement.

They continue making sausage. While Rosemarie concentrates on size, John carries on with a task he's been doing his whole life. "What was it you wanted to talk about?" he asks.

"Oh, I nearly forgot. I'm pregnant."

John drops the casing. The grinder continues to churn out meat. "Wow!" he exclaims, shutting off the machine just as the mixer bowl threatens to overflow. There's no confusing John's reaction. It's joyful. "That's fantastic, Rosie! Wow, I'm gonna be a father!" John shouts.

"There's more, John."

"I know. It'll keep," John says, glancing at the ground pork.

"I'm not sure who the father is," Rosemarie admits.

John's smile dissolves into a blank expression.

"Before you ask, I'll just tell you. Frankie and I... "

"I knew it."

"Wait! It was a mistake. We both agreed it was a terrible drunken mistake. And I promise you, John, it will never happen again. I told you, we're just friends."

Rosemarie waits for John to say something. She can see that he's thinking though his countenance remains indecipherable. He dumps the bowl of meat back into the hopper and extricates the spent casing. John grabs both of Rosemarie's hands. "I don't care,

Rose. I don't care if Frankie's the father. I'll love it just the same. I mean it."

Rosemarie wasn't expecting that. *Jesus, that makes the next bit tricky.* "I was also offered the HR job at the hotel. I don't know what I'm going to do," Rosemarie says.

John doesn't hesitate. "That's great, Rose," he says, although Rosemarie gets the impression that he doesn't mean it. "Lookit, it doesn't matter where you work, or what you do. I'll be there for you and the baby."

Jesus, Mary and Joseph! Is this guy for real? "John, listen... don't get too far ahead of yourself. I can't very well work full-time and raise a kid. I'm thinking of terminating the pregnancy."

John deflates like a punctured airhole in a sausage. "Oh," he says.

"I just found out, so I haven't decided. But I have to give the hotel people an answer."

"Don't do it, Rose. *Please.*" John says this so softly that Rosemarie can barely hear him. "I mean, go ahead and take the job if that's what you want to do. Just please don't–" John's eyes fill with tears.

Rosemarie shucks off her smock and throws it into the bin marked, "soiled." She washes her hands and puts her sweater and jacket on. John hasn't said another word to her. She can't stand to look at his anguished expression. She can't imagine what he's thinking. She whispers, "Goodnight, John," and leaves him to finish the job. She walks home in the dark. If anyone were to see Rosemarie they wouldn't be able to tell if those were tears of sorrow or joy. She's not sure herself.

When Rosemarie gets home she's still in a trance. She doesn't notice Frankie watching her climb the stairs. When Rosemarie reaches the top, Frankie sees that she's been crying and asks, "What's wrong, sugar?"

"Oh, Frankie. It's a mess! My life's a mess!" Rosemarie blubbers, and falls into his arms sobbing.

"There, there, Rose. Calm down. Shhhh," Frankie says, rubbing her back. "Tell me what's wrong."

"I'm pregnant and I got the job and John loves me and I made sausage and I should get an abortion and John loves me and... Oh, God, Frankie. It could be yours!"

"No it can't, Rose. Nothing happened that night."

"What?"

"I'm not into necrophilia, even though it was Halloween."

"Necro what? What do you mean, Frankie?"

"I don't do corpses. You passed out."

"You mean... "

"That's right. Nothing happened, even though you were gagging for it. I'm not the father."

"Oh, Frankie!" Rosemarie shouts. "It's John's!"

"And John loves you," Frankie reminds her.

"You knew?"

"Of course, I knew. Everyone knows. Even Mervin knows, for crying out loud. Don't you know how hard it was for me to not... you know. And Timo, too. It was very hard for him to walk away. Everyone knows John is smitten."

"Except me, apparently."

"Love is blind, eh?" Frankie says.

When Bernard returns Rosemarie's phone call, he tells her that she had the whole team cracking up over some crazy answer she gave at her interview about not knowing what her long term goals are. "That's a good one, Princess," Bernard says. "You really threw them off until they realised you were having them on. Congratulations."

"It's true," Rosemarie says. "I don't know."

"Oh, come on... you don't expect me to believe that."

"Believe what you want. I don't know where I see myself tomorrow, let alone next year. I'm pregnant," Rosemarie confesses and waits for the shit to hit the proverbial fan.

She has to wait a good long while. Bernard puts her on hold. He comes back and says, "Look, *Rose*. I've got another call. Let me know what you decide to do." Bernard sounds pissed. "And don't take forever, I put my neck on the line for you."

"Wait, Bernard... what do you mean, you put your neck—" Too late, the dial tone indicates he took the other call.

So, it seems that becoming the successful candidate has more to do with Bernard than Rosemarie. *It Figures*. That's how the real world works. Rosemarie's been living in some dream world where she was under the impression that her education, experience and skills were what mattered. Apparently not.

Rosemarie has had a lot of surprises this week. She should stop being so presumptuous and wake up. It's who you know.

She wastes no more time deciding what to do. Rosemarie calls Golden Daffodil's blooming flunky and tells him that she's accepted another offer. She doesn't even bother to say thanks.

On the first truly warm day of spring, Rosemarie lounges in a lawn chair under a budding sugar maple tree in the backyard. Her feet are elevated on a milk crate. Doctor's orders. She browses through an old copy of *Name Your Baby*, looking for inspiration. John brings Rosemarie a little bottle of Orangina. He kisses Rosemarie on the top of her head and settles down on the grass beside her.

John looks up at the buds that will soon form a canopy of green. He tells Rosemarie the story of his dad and uncle fighting over the sapling they dug up on Mount McKay, although John wasn't around to witness it. "Lina told me about a battle that raged between my dad and Uncle Francis over where to plant it. They finally reached a compromise and planted it in the exact centre of the backyard, before they even finished building the house. It's older than me," John says.

Rosemarie puts down the book and takes a sip of Orangina. "What about Conrad if it's a boy? Or Barbara, if it's a girl—Conrad Black's wife. Your mother would be tickled pink."

"I don't know, Rosie. One woman with expensive taste in the household is enough."

John goes back into the house and returns a moment later with a FedEx package. "Here," he says. "This is for you. I figured you might like to pick out your own ring when the swelling in your fingers goes down." John rests the package down and picks up Rosemarie's left hand. He kisses each of her five little sausages. "Consider this an engagement present."

John didn't take more than a breath to say yes when Rosemarie asked him to make an honest woman out of her and marry her. Rosemarie is adamant; anything but a shotgun wedding at the Italian Hall. John said he doesn't care where or when, as long as she will have him.

Rosemarie rips open the box and her jaw drops.

"Oh, my God! Jimmy Choo sling-backs!" she squeals with delight. "How did you know?"

"Frankie."

"But my feet are swollen worse than my fingers," Rosemarie protests. "They won't fit."

"Yeah, but they will after the baby is born and your feet return to normal. Meanwhile, you can dangle them from your ring finger."

"Engagement shoes! I love you, Johnny Falcone."

"Johnny Falcone loves Rosie Catanzaro. Look," John says. He points to the base of the maple tree. "There's the proof." *JF hearts RC* is carved into the trunk.

Rosemarie is flabbergasted. "When did you do that?

"Grade six."

The Flying Catanzaro

When Rosemarie told John she decided not to take the HR job, he looked very pleased. When she told John she decided to keep the baby, she could tell he was over-the-moon. Rosemarie continued to work part-time in the meat department until she could no longer handle it physically. By the time that smock fit her, Rosemarie had become a competent sausage maker.

Lina turned out to be very competent at the computer. She is now implementing an integrated inventory control system which will speed up reordering stock and automatically cost the inventory. Lina is confident that it will enable them to print accurate and timely financial reports. She looks forward to an improvement in efficiency by their next fiscal year-end.

Lina promised to keep working until after the baby is born. She is eager to retire when Rosemarie is ready to take over her duties full-time. Lina claims the only reason she could not consider retirement until now, is because when the next cash carrying *paesano* can't find her, they could be robbed by their own staff. With the computer keeping track of the stock, Lina will be able to tell if anything goes astray. "Besides," Lina said with deep regret, "there's not too many old boys with a pocket full of cash anymore. We're living in a cash-less society. Goddamn banks!"

When Nick's girlfriend, Deedee refused his marriage proposal, Nick asked if he could move into Rosemarie's apartment when she moved in with John. Nick and Deedee didn't break up. Deedee says she's too old to change her ways and likes things just the way they are; with separate houses. Nick discovered he doesn't like living alone, and Frankie is the best roommate Nick could ever wish for.

Rosemarie has come to terms with moving. She finally realised that her dad comes with *her*, not the building. And she can always visit whenever she wants.

Lina took over Nick and Frankie's side of the duplex. The twins fixed up Lina's old sewing room and redecorated it as a nursery. Rosemarie didn't have to give up her lake view. She brought her favourite chair with her and witnessed the arrival of the ice breaker. The *Samuel Risley* heralded the beginning of the shipping season and Rosemarie's third trimester. Rosemarie is content to spend the rest of her pregnancy enjoying the view from her perch in the attic.

The Falcones were flying back and forth switching places like a trapeze act. *The Flying Catanzaro: Nick releases Frankie. Frankie flies to Rosemarie. Rosemarie flies to John while Nick flies to Frankie. Lina flies over the cuckoos nest and lands on her own two feet. Only the catcher never moves.*

Rosemarie came up with a scheme for John to buy-out Frankie's shares. John is paying Frankie in installments in lieu of his regular pay cheques while Frankie attends Master Locks Academy of Hair Design. Rosemarie suggested John replace Frankie with a revolving group of part-time workers collectively known as the Unwed Mothers. Rosemarie recruited, hired and trained them herself. The Unwed Mothers work the maximum hours that are allowable without jeopardising their benefits. They babysit for each other while they're at work in the meat department earning a little extra cash. They're gaining valuable experience to put on the résumés Rosemarie is helping them to write. Dawn, formerly known as Autumn Dawn, is working out very well. Sandy, formerly known as

Candy, moved to Toronto when her x-boyfriend and bad-ass biker was sent to prison.

Dawn offered to babysit for Rosemarie when the baby arrives, but Lina says she's got that covered. In fact Lina has been enjoying babysitting for Dawn. Lina watches Amber while Dawn attends evening classes to earn a high school equivalency certificate.

There will be no shortage of babysitters for Rosemarie and John's baby. All four of Roseanna's daughters are eager to spend time with their new cousin. They're all praying for a boy.

Roseanna says she is looking forward to Eddie's next "furlough." She says it's about time she got some action, too. Roseanna told Eddie if he doesn't get home soon, she might pick up her little sister's bad habit and call up a couple of his cousins.

Rosemarie's mother continues to make donations to the casino. She is thrilled that her youngest daughter is finally going to produce a child, and even more thrilled with her future son-in-law. She feeds him *bagna cauda* whenever she can.

Timo has taken on an apprentice. He says he'll continue to work until the new butcher is fully trained. Timo told John he'll cover for him anytime he wants to spend some quality time with his kid. Rosemarie introduced Timo to her best friend, Jen. She hasn't seen either of them since.

Gord continues to drive Lina to the bank everyday. Lina makes regular deposits into her personal savings account, a few hundred dollars at a time. If anyone were to ask, she'd say she won it at the casino. It was Lina's idea to send Frankie to "beauty school," as she insists on calling it. She paid Frankie's tuition with the "education fund" she had been secretly squirrelling away for years.

Epilogue

On the second day of August, while the first shipment of tomatoes from Southwestern Ontario is being delivered to Falcone Fine Foods, Rosemarie delivers a healthy baby girl weighing approximately the same as a *soppressata piquante,* and just as precious. The tomatoes are early, but the baby isn't.

They name her Connie in deference to where she was conceived.

Acknowledgments

I am eternally grateful to Northwestern Ontario Writers' Workshop for connecting me with LUNA members Glenn Ponka, Sue Blott, Joan Baril, Nancy Bjorgo and Jacqueline D'acre. Without their expert guidance you would not be reading this, or I'd be doing time.

Thanks to Pam Horosco, Ivan Jefferis, Ulla Poulson and Laura Macgowan for their solicited opinions and unfettered responses.

What a delight it's been to work with Sandra Preisig at Fidel Productions. Sandra's "acrobatic" skills and impeccable timing achieve high marks for artistic impression and technical merit.

I am so lucky to have the love and support of Sherry Anne Kelly, who taught me that laughter for its own sake is therapeutic, and even better just for the hell of it.

My husband has suffered greatly during the creative process that usurped meals, household chores and so much more. Countless nights of disturbed sleep while I prowled in search of a verb and a pencil can never be replaced, nor repaid. Thanks, PW.

www.ingramcontent.com/pod-product-compliance
Lightning Source LLC
Chambersburg PA
CBHW031946240626

47153CB00003B/876